THE MONTH
OF THE
FALLING
LEAVES

THE MONTH
OF THE
FALLING
LEAVES

a novel by

Bruce Marshall

DOUBLEDAY & COMPANY, INC.

GARDEN CITY, NEW YORK, 1963

All of the characters in this book are fictitious, and any resemblance to actual persons, living or dead, is purely coincidental.

LIBRARY OF CONGRESS CATALOG CARD NUMBER 63–11235
COPYRIGHT © 1963 BY BRUCE MARSHALL
ALL RIGHTS RESERVED
PRINTED IN THE UNITED STATES OF AMERICA
FIRST EDITION IN THE UNITED STATES OF AMERICA

For

MORRIS WEST

Author's Note

In the course of thirty years I have employed several literary agents to hawk my wares. None of them resembled Catacomb and none ever tried to take advantage of official but unrealistic rates of foreign exchange.

Immediately after the second world war I served on the same Inter-Allied Commission as a distinguished Civil Servant who ultimately became British Ambassador in Warsaw and from whom I received nothing but kindness. "Nodder" is drawn neither from him nor from any of his predecessors or successors and is introduced into the novel solely because my plot required an Ambassador.

Indeed the only character in this story not entirely imaginary is Wanda, whom I once glimpsed hurtling up a hotel stairway in Barcelona.

B. M.

"Mais il est des villes et des pays où les gens ont, de temps en temps, le soupçon d'autre chose. En général, cela ne change pas leur vie. Seulement il y a eu le soupçon et c'est toujours cela de gagné."

ALBERT CAMUS: *La Peste*

THE MONTH
OF THE
FALLING
LEAVES

1

"*Chatterley of the Apes, Lady Tarzan's Lover*, sex and adventure, they're the money spinners—Harold." The Christian name slid through the tubby literary agent's whipcord lips discreetly, like a prune stone he was ashamed to be seen discarding. "There's no future in philosophy."

"Fifty thousand copies isn't so dusty surely." Catacomb could call Hilliard Harold till he was blue in the face, Hilliard wasn't going to debase intimacy by calling Catacomb Cuthbert.

"Fifty thousand copies in *Poland,* nine hundred and seventeen in *England.* And the little the Poles pay they try to avoid remitting by saying that the National Bank of Poland won't cough up the sterling. So it's not a bad idea of yours to cash in in zlotys while you're over there on this lecture jaunt. If you'll give me a minute or two I'll work out our commission: nineteen percent of course, as it's a foreign sale—nine percent for us, ten percent for Gumshott."

"Who's Gumshott?"

"Our man in Warsaw who lives in Putney, but he speaks the language like a native—in fact no bother at all."

While Catacomb scribbled away on a pad, Hilliard did another kind of calculation in his head. If Poles were as mean about buying books as his fellow countrymen, a sale of fifty thousand copies of *The Symphony of Discord* in Poland meant that a million Poles had made an effort to understand the Dysteleological Surd. Apart from his own bored students Hilliard hadn't met ten Britons who had ever heard of the Dysteleological Surd, let alone known that it was the name

1

given by Edgar Sheffield Brightman to the unmerited sufferings of men and animals which seemed to disprove the existence of a benevolent Creator. A million readers! Small wonder that the Towarzystwo Metafizyczne w Warszawie had invited him to fly over to Poland and lecture to its members.

Catacomb tilted the pad towards Hilliard.

"Fifty thousand, one hundred and seventeen copies at thirty zlotys makes 1,503,510 zlotys. Royalty at seven percent on 1,503,510 zlotys 105,245 zlotys. Commission at nineteen percent thereon 19,996 zlotys. However that still leaves you the whole 105,245 zlotys to play around with in Warsaw night clubs as naturally you'll be settling our commission in sterling — £298 : 9 : 0 at the official rate of sixty-seven zlotys to the pound. No hurry of course. You can let us have your check in due course. Make it out to Catacomb and Priddle and we'll send Gumshott his whack."

It wasn't until he was out in the street that Hilliard realized that he had allowed Catacomb to pull a fast one on him. Charlotte would never forgive him. Charlotte would point out that if a Professor of Logic and Metaphysics at a red brick university could be expected to spend 105,245 zlotys in ten days in Warsaw night clubs, a couple of literary agents could have been told to go over and spend 19,996 zlotys in them in three. Charlotte would remind him that apart from his £100 in traveler's checks, luckily unlikely to be required, he had only £148 in the bank. But a bargain was a bargain: now that he had been coward enough to accept Catacomb's demand for sterling he would have to trust to being able to sell his surplus zlotys in London at a rate that wasn't too unfavourable.

When he lined up next morning at the air terminal to have his ticket checked and his luggage weighed, Hilliard found that he was the only Briton in a long line of shabby Slavs with eyes as filmy as lavatory windows. After he had finished with these formalities he went and bought a *Daily Telegraph*, and turning to walk away from the newsstand bumped into a young Pole with stainless steel teeth who grinned at him and said:

2

" 'He who ne'er deigns his Bible to peruse
  Would deem it hard to be denied his news.'

Crabbe, I think—the poet of course, not the frogman."

Never good at conversation with strangers even when they
were erudite, Hilliard was relieved when one of the clips of his
new braces gave and the necessity of adjusting it in the lavatory provided him with an excuse for leaving the young man.
The braces had been bought at the same time as his black
raglan overcoat. Charlotte had said that with clip braces he
wouldn't be bothered with having to sew on buttons if any of
them worked loose while he was in Warsaw, and he had been
too frightened of hurting her feelings to ask her to pack an
ordinary pair for security.

When the coach was announced, Hilliard was the last to
board it. As the young man with the steel teeth was sitting alone
in a double seat at the back, Hilliard went and sat in another
unoccupied double seat at the front. The noise of the engine
wasn't loud enough to drown his neighbors' conversation, but
since he didn't understand what they were saying he was able
to believe that it was intelligent. The pavements were crowded
with office workers hurrying to their unrecordable activities.
Hilliard didn't think that even Pepys would have been able to
give life to their spiritless faces born to be photographed
gaping.

Admiral Sir David Doddick's face however was of the
assertive type and the *Daily Telegraph's* picture of him shaking
General de Gaulle's frosty fin on the steps of the Elysée had
caught the thrust of the famous jaw. The Admiral, the *Daily
Telegraph* said, had been paying a courtesy visit to the French
President in order to recall wartime experiences. Sandwiched
in between advertisements of young women in the bleak
scaffoldings of modern corsetry, the *Daily Telegraph* had also
news about ducks' eggs and Mr. Macmillan, but Hilliard didn't
bother to read it. At fifty, Hilliard had already received what
Arnold Bennett's biographer calls "one of time's taps on the

shoulder" and was finding that it hurt his eyes to look at small print in swiftly moving vehicles.

The strips of office workers were quickly left behind and soon the bus was rushing past a filibuster of banal villas and women pushing perambulators. Afraid that the other passengers might neglect to do so, Hilliard waved back to a group of children in a garden.

"There is perhaps more in that encounter than meets the eye." To Hilliard's displeasure the young Pole with the steel teeth had come forward to sit beside him and was pointing at the photograph of the Admiral and General de Gaulle in the *Daily Telegraph* still open on his knee.

"Of course there isn't. We're not as devious as that—more's the pity." Hilliard wanted to sound discouraging. "The Admiral's an old sailor. The General's an old soldier. What more natural than that he and Tomato should want to get together again and discuss their wartime experiences?"

"Tomato—so you know the Admiral then?"

"Of course I don't. What on earth's put that idea into your head?"

"Then if you do not know the Admiral why do you call him by his nickname?"

"It's a habit we have in England when people are famous. Everybody calls Montgomery Monty. Everybody calls Doddick Tomato." Hilliard had in fact once been spoken to by the Admiral, but he saw no reason why he should tell the Pole. The Admiral and he had been sitting in adjacent chairs in the smoking room of the Athenaeum. Hilliard had been reading *The Hibbert Journal* and the Admiral *Men Only*. "Looks as though it's going to keep up for Lords," the Admiral had said to Hilliard as he had got up and walked away.

"You yourself were in the Navy during the war perhaps?" said the young Pole.

"No."

"In the Infantry then?"

"No."

4

"In the Royal Air Force perhaps?"

"Look, shall we just say that I did my duty?"

"I understand. Hush-hush?"

"Rush-rush—Royal Army Pay Corps in other words."

"In that case you must be a mathematician."

"On the contrary I'm a philosopher."

"Wittgenstein says that there can be no valid system of philosophy which is not based on mathematics and science."

"In that case Wittgenstein will just have to consider me a bad philosopher."

"Philosophers must no longer have their heads in the air. Philosophers must have their foots on the ground."

"Feet," Hilliard corrected sharply and was immediately ashamed of himself. What right had he who did not know a single word of Polish to snub the young man for a trivial mistake in English? To atone for his waspishness he said: "You're quite right though. My wife's always telling me that I'm not nearly practical enough."

"My wife also helps me with her counsels and deliberations. The family is a small island of fidelity, I think. If there is no fidelity in the family there can be no fidelity in the nation."

"I couldn't agree with you more."

"In London many girls endeavoured to entice me from the small island of fidelity on which I live with my wife, but because I knew that my wife was being as true as gold to me in Warsaw I remained as true as gold to her in London and I sent the enticing girls away with a flea in their ear."

"That does you credit." Hilliard had always remained on a small island of fidelity with Charlotte—red brick provided as little accommodation for adultery as an escalator—but he was by no means sure that Charlotte had always remained on a small island of fidelity with him. Charlotte had been pretty when she was young and there had been that embalmer at Torquay in 1937 and those two unused tickets in her dressing table drawer for the *Messiah* which she had been supposed to have attended in his company.

"I do not expect however that the Admiral Tomato has always lived on a small island of fidelity with the Lady Tomato. I expect that the Admiral Tomato had a Lady Tomato in every port."

"When he was young perhaps, who knows?"

"I think that it is very pleasant to be young. I think that your Admiral Tomato thought so too. I think that when your Admiral Tomato was young it diverted him greatly to lie and bask in the sunny climes of the south with multitudes of Lady Tomatoes."

"No doubt." Tired of listening to the young Pole's nonsense, Hilliard began to go over in his head the packing he had done that morning in his hotel bedroom to make sure that he had left nothing out as Charlotte had foretold that he would. Charlotte had been wrong: he had forgotten to pack neither his sponge bag nor his pajamas nor the nail-clippers which he had purchased in Boots before Linguistic Analysis had been invented and which had already outlasted Hitler's Reich and the French Fourth Republic. What he *had* forgotten to do however was to lock his suitcase after he had packed it. This was an omission which was going to be difficult to remedy if, as generally happened these days, there were no customs examination and the passengers' luggage were loaded straight on to the plane from the bus. But, provided the porters weren't too brisk, there was just a chance that he would be able to lock the suitcase when they arrived at the airport.

His luck was in. Although he was by no means among the first off the bus, when he ran round to the back he saw the brown Revelation Charlotte had bought for him in Selfridge's lying on top of an unattended barrow. As he was about to fit the key into the first lock to fasten the clasp his arms were seized from behind and he was pulled round to face a fretsaw of gleaming steel teeth.

"Why do you attempt to burgle my suitcase?" the young Pole asked angrily.

"It's not your suitcase; it's mine." Flustered, Hilliard bent to read the name on the luggage label which the Pole was holding out for his inspection: to his dismay it was KARMINSKI.

"Perhaps now you will believe me." The Pole was still quivering with rage.

"I'm terribly sorry, but I could have sworn it was mine." Hilliard drew the Pole's attention to a second brown Revelation being stacked by a porter on top of another barrow. "You can see for yourself, can't you? As like as two peas. On the bus on the way down I suddenly remembered I'd forgotten to lock mine, but naturally I ought to have had the sense to look at the label first."

To Hilliard's astonishment the young Pole ran across to the second barrow and pressed each clasp on the other Revelation.

"Yes," he said when both clasps had sprung open, "you had forgotten to lock it all right."

"Good Lord! Do you mean to say you didn't believe me?"

"Anyway I believe you now and that's what matters. And now if you will be so kind as to give me your key I shall be happy to atone for having been a doubting Thomas by securely locking your suitcase for you."

"Thanks, but I prefer to do it myself." Hilliard took longer over the operation than was necessary so as not to have to walk into the airport with the Pole, and in the waiting room he avoided his company ostentatiously.

2

The plane was Polish and had POLSKIE LINIE LOTNICZE
painted on it in red letters. Although among the last to climb
the gangway, Hilliard was again lucky enough to get a double
seat to himself in the middle. When he turned round to watch
where the stewardess was hanging his overcoat he saw that
Karminski was sitting at the back with another young Pole
whom Hilliard didn't remember having seen either in the coach
or the waiting room. This second young Pole's face looked so
hard and unfriendly that Hilliard wondered whether he might
not be some sort of security policeman—if BOAC flew publishers impressively might not POLSKIE LINIE LOTNICZE fly
foreigners suspiciously? Had Karminski been telling him
about how he had caught Hilliard trying to fit a key into his
suitcase outside the airport? If so there was nothing Hilliard
could do about it: the plane was now taxying along the runway
and already he was as good as behind the Iron Curtain where
the protection afforded by a British passport was as illusory as
in Douglas, Isle of Man.

Gradually however the normality of the rows of conceited
and misshapen heads in front of him, the English, German
and Polish NO SMOKING and FASTEN YOUR SAFETY BELT signs,
and the Esperanto of the air hostess's unpinchable little bottom
reassured Hilliard and helped him to forget about Karminski
and his friend. Soon the plane had been lifted off the land
which was spread out under it in unreal relief, fields and houses
shrunken into postage stamps and weather Darby-and-Joans,
and miniscule cars creeping along invisible veins of roads like
dinky toys. Might it not be this view of a diminished universe,

Hilliard conjectured, which was the explanation of God's apparent unconcern for all the pain and loneliness rolling round and round underneath Him? The conceit, he quickly saw, was untenable: God, if He existed, was neither up nor down nor alongside. When Hilliard next looked out of his porthole they were over the frail sea, fluttering in the wind like a girl's silk dress.

"You travel to East Berlin or to Warsaw?" To Hilliard's surprise Karminski had come forward to sit beside him again and his expression was as friendly as though the mistake about the suitcase had never occurred.

"To Warsaw."

"Warsaw is a noble town. I think that you will like it. Do you speak Polish?"

"Not a word, I'm ashamed to say, but I hope to be able to rub along with my German."

"German is not a wise language to speak in Poland. French is much wiser. Do you speak French?"

"Very much better than German. German's the worst of my languages."

"And what are the other foreign languages which you know how to speak?"

"Italian and Spanish but I mix them up rather."

"For an Englishman you speak many foreign languages— too many for it to have been fitting that you should have been a soldier in the Rush-rush."

"Armies are like that. The German army too—fortunately for us, otherwise we mightn't have won the war."

"I do not know very much about those things. When the war was in Poland I was too young to fight."

"Of course. I ought to have realized." At fifty it was only wrinkles and not the degree of their absence that a man could assess. Alamein was already in the mists with Hill 60 and Flodden, and a new generation of thugs and their victims had grown up. With memory at the mercy of physiology what hope was there for the "just and lasting peace" the politicians kept prating about?

"You are wondering perhaps where I learned my excellent English. I learned my excellent English at our Polish Embassy in London. I have been many times attached to our Polish Embassy in London."

"So you are a diplomat are you, Mr. Karminski?"

When Karminski only smiled instead of answering, Hilliard's distrust of him returned. It was notorious that Soviet Russia and her satellites used their embassies as conning towers and spies were the first to suspect others of spying on them. Was that why Karminski hadn't taken Hilliard's word for it that he had forgotten to lock his suitcase and rushed across to test the clasps for himself—because he had imagined that Hilliard was some sort of M.I.5 agent trying to have another clumsy Western peep? Was Karminski quite sure about him yet? Had his remark that Hilliard spoke too many foreign languages for a soldier in the Rush-rush been an insinuation that Hilliard had served in the Hush-hush and probably still did?

"Perhaps it is good that you do not speak Polish. Like that when a pretty girl in Warsaw says 'no' you will be able to imagine that she has said 'yes' and it will be very pleasant for you." Karminski seemed to have forgotten what he had said in the bus about small islands of fidelity. "Is this your first trip to Poland?"

"It is."

"Then there are many things which you must know about our country. And the first thing that you must know is how to obtain quickly a drink." Turning round, Karminski scratched his Adam's apple with his forefinger and within less than a minute the stewardess had brought a bottle of vodka and two small glasses. Karminski filled both glasses and handed one to Hilliard. *"Hop siup!* That is how we say mud-in-your-eye in Polish."

Was this an attempt to woo him into careless talk? After a

sip or two of the vodka Hilliard was almost able to giggle at the thought: the lowdown on Royal Army Pay Corps procedure could only help the East to lose a hot war, not win one.

"The second thing which you must know about our country is that it is a political democracy in which the many are not exploited for the few. Gomulka is not like Franco."

"I had heard rumors."

"Pigs for instance. In 1919 five and a half million pigs were raised in Poland; in 1958 twelve million pigs. It is the same with steel. In 1913 one thousand six hundred and sixty-seven million tons of steel; in 1958 five thousand six hundred and thirty-one million tons of steel. However we must also proclaim our faults. The increase of the girls in the bars of Warsaw since the October revolution in 1956 has been almost as great in proportion as the increase in the pigs and in the steel. Since October girls I call them, but I do not think they have been as good for our country as the pigs and the steel, although perhaps for the Western capitalists they are better."

Hilliard agreed. The answer for the West, he thought muzzily, was *ballets roses* in the Kremlin and golf at Odessa. Either that or the Moderator of the Free Kirk of Scotland commuting between 10 Downing Street and the White House.

"Now we drink the other half," Karminski said as he refilled both glasses.

They kept the bottle with them during lunch and by the time they touched down to refuel in Schönefeld in East Berlin, Hilliard was wondering how he could ever have been so stupid as to imagine that a nice man like Karminski could have taken him for an M.I.5 snooper.

Because the hostess was busy helping other passengers into their overcoats, Hilliard took his raglan off the hanger himself. An official in a khaki uniform with green epaulettes gave him a friendly smile as he handed him his transit pass and DEUTSCHE DEMOKRATISCHE REPUBLIK in monster blue capitals across the brown facade of the airport looked much less sinister than Hilliard was going to pretend to his colleagues when he returned. The frowsy waiting room into which the transit passengers were herded was as peacefully undialectic as the lavatory whither Hilliard hurried to fasten his refractory brace clips. When he came out he found Karminski and the policeman-like Pole waiting at the door.

"My friend here is afraid that you may have put on his overcoat instead of your own," Karminski said.

Two glances were enough: the overcoat the other Pole was holding out for his inspection was Hilliard's black raglan, that which Hilliard was wearing, a midnight blue exactly like the one Charlotte had said he was too old for. When he had taken the overcoat off, Hilliard showed the Pole the maker's tag.

"Mine's an Aquascutum too and in the darkness at the back of the plane. . . ."

"Please. It is nothing."

But Hilliard noticed that as soon as Karminski's friend had put the midnight blue raglan on, he felt carefully in both pockets; and when the two Poles walked over to the coffee counter they didn't invite Hilliard to join them.

3

The plane took off again at twenty-five past three and rose swiftly from a ragged field into a smudgy sky. Karminski was again sitting with his policeman-like friend at the back, and this disturbed Hilliard. Within a space of a few hours he had been caught trying to fit his key into Karminski's suitcase and with Karminski's friend's overcoat on his back: two blunders like that committed on top of one another were perhaps too much for the representatives of a humorless régime to ascribe to chance. He was relieved therefore when Karminski came forward again and sat down in the empty seat beside him.

"Łódź." Karminski pointed out through the window at a distant jumble of houses and towers. "The center of Poland's textile industry. Sixty hundred and ninety-six thousand inhabitants and only .002 percent of them Since October girls. Please, my friend asks me to tell you that he beseeches you not to worry about having taken his overcoat. My friend and I are like brothers and that is why I know that you can believe him when he asserts that he knows that it was by mistake that you have taken his overcoat by mistake. Please, I do not wish to appear as curious as a cat, but for how long are you staying in our capital city?"

"Ten days, that's all your London consulate would give me." Deciding that showing he had nothing to hide might very well be the best way of convincing Karminski and his policeman-like friend that they had nothing to discover, Hilliard opened his passport at the Polish visa stamp and handed it to Karminski. "*Listopada*'s November, I take it?"

"*Of* November. Genitive of *Listopad* which in Polish means the month of the falling leaves."

"But that's poetry!" Hilliard exclaimed with pleasure and concluded that his second set of fears had been as unfounded as his first: a nation that could name a month so enchantingly could not possibly fly secret police in plain clothes on its airlines.

"And December, what do you call it? The month of the falling snow?"

"The month of the frozen ground. All our months have names of surpassing beauty. If you like I shall write them down for you." Karminski tore a page from a notebook and wrote on it with Hilliard's passport underneath as a pad.

January, the month of the forest of encounter, October, the month of preparing flax, were the names which Hilliard liked best on the list Karminski gave him.

"You are a great traveler, I see, Professor Hilliard," Karminski said as he handed back the passport which he had apparently been examining in detail while Hilliard had been reading through the Polish months and their translations.

"From necessity: my profession obliges me to attend educational conferences all over the world."

"And that is the reason of your visit to Warsaw—to attend an educational conference?"

"No; this time my purpose is slightly more personal: I have been invited to give a lecture to the Warsaw Metaphysical Society." Even his Polish fame, it seemed, was only relative. A million Poles who had read his book, still left twenty-nine million Poles who hadn't. Karminski must be one of them, otherwise he would have recognized Hilliard's name.

For perhaps the hundred and forty-seventh time the hostess trudged up the aisle. The hostess was beginning to look tired —and a tuck of her white silk blouse had worked loose from the top of her skirt. Hilliard gave her a smile of sympathy as she came clumping down again and the hostess grinned back comically.

"You are like my father, I see," Karminski said. "Although he is seventy and has to use spectacles to read he never needs

14

to put them on his nose to recognize when girls are as pretty as paint. I do not think that the girls whom the Warsaw Metaphysical Society will send to greet you at the airport at Okecie will be as pretty as paint. I think that they will be blue stocking girls with black moustaches."

Black moustaches or not, Hilliard doubted whether the blue stocking girls of the Warsaw Metaphysical Society would be impressed with his competence to explain the Dysteleological Surd were his trousers to fall down as soon as he got off the plane, so he went to the lavatory and made sure that his brace clips were holding properly. When he returned, the vodka bottle and the two small glasses were back again.

"Before we land we must drink mud-in-your-eye to your lecture, Professor Hilliard."

"All right. But this time the drinks are on me—the hostess will be able to cash a traveler's check for me, I presume?"

"The hostess will not be able to cash a traveler's check for you. Only the Narodowy Bank Polski or a hotel authorized by the Narodowy Bank Polski can cash traveler's checks. The Narodowy Bank Polski requires foreign currency reserves and it cannot allow any chance of building them up to slip through its fingers. However, if you really wish to buy me a drink I shall be only too pleased to call on you at your hotel. At which hotel will you be staying during your sojourn in Warsaw?"

"At the Leningrad."

"In that case I shall pay a visit to you at the Leningrad. *Hop siup!* Let us hope that you will speak eloquently and persuasively to the blue stocking girls with the black moustaches of the Warsaw Metaphysical Society."

Karminski had barely paid the stewardess when the safety belt and no smoking notices lighted up again. Far underneath the plane the earth tilted like a huge green saucer tipped towards the mouth of an invisible cat. Hilliard closed his eyes until he felt the reassuring roll of wheels and he made sure that the overcoat which the stewardess brought him was his own before he put it on.

"And I shall give you this in order that you may not make your third mistake of the day and take mine," Karminski said as he handed Hilliard his briefcase. "Professor Hilliard, I am enchanted to have made the acquaintance of a distinguished British philosopher."

"And I to have made that of a distinguished Polish diplomat." But Hilliard's mind was only half on what he was saying. What if the Warsaw Metaphysical Society had forgotten to send even a blue stocking girl with a black moustache to greet him? And if there were no branch of the Narodowy Bank Polski at the airport, where was he going to find the zlotys to pay for the coach to the terminal and a taxi from the terminal to the hotel?

He need not have worried. As soon as he appeared at the top of the steps, there was a roar of cheering from a choir of faces waiting on the tarmac. Magnesium bulbs flashed and handkerchiefs fluttered. All that seemed to be missing was a guard of honor to inspect and a band. The Dysteleological Surd had come into its own at last.

4

Television and newsreel photographers were churning away as Hilliard walked down the steps. When he reached the bottom, a girl who certainly hadn't a black moustache thrust a microphone at his mouth.

"Professor Hilliard, will you be so kind as to address a few words of greeting to the Polish nation."

"I am very happy to be here. I am honored that my book should have been so widely read in your country." Hilliard began to sympathize with peripatetic statesmen: talking sense off the cuff to the faceless millions was far from being as easy as he had imagined.

"Professor Hilliard, will you please impart to the people of Poland your opinions about peaceful co-existence."

"I think that peaceful co-existence is possible provided the East learns to trust the West and the West learns to trust the East." Macmillan, Kennedy, Khrushchev, when it came to the Delphic balderdash, he could be as obscure as the best of them.

"Professor Hilliard, will you please confide to the people of Poland your estimate of the novels of Miss Iris Murdoch."

"I think that Miss Iris Murdoch's novels are excellent." They must be: Charlotte never read them.

Even Karminski and his policeman-like friend had stopped to gawk and the other passengers were smiling with the oozy deference of Hilliard's colleagues watching the Duke of Edinburgh confer honorary degrees. Because he was already holding bouquets offered by the *Trybuna Ludu* and the *Zycie Warszawy,* Hilliard dropped a third presented by the *Nowa Wies,* but he was the hero of the minute and the laughter was

17

kindly. Soon Witkowski, his publisher, was carrying ten bouquets for him.

By the time the official speeches were over, the interest of Hilliard's fellow passengers had evaporated, and when Witkowski was at last able to lead him into the customs shed they had vanished, and Hilliard's brown Revelation was the only piece of luggage left on the counter. The porter tore off the tag without bothering to compare it with Hilliard's half. The customs officer stamped Hilliard's foreign currency import declaration without even glancing at the amounts inscribed and when he had chalked the suitcase, asked if Hilliard would be kind enough to autograph his copy of *Symfonia Dysonansów*.

"You see now how many readers you have in Poland," Witkowski said. "Polish people are very deeply interested in philosophy."

"So it would seem." Who, Hilliard thought, could imagine one of Her Majesty's Nosey Parkers at Dover producing a copy of *Language, Truth and Logic* for A. J. Ayer to sign?

"I think that your stay in Poland will be pleasurable," Witkowski said as he led Hilliard out through more cheers and waves to a car. "There is however, a fly in the ointment. The British Ambassador has informed the Metaphysical Society that he regrets that he will be unable to attend your lecture tomorrow evening as he is leaving Warsaw to spend a few days in the country. The officials of the British Council have also informed the Metaphysical Society that they regret that they will be unable to attend your lecture tomorrow evening as they too are leaving Warsaw to spend a few days in the country. No doubt the British Ambassador and the officials of the British Council are spending their few days in the country together."

"No doubt." But Hilliard thought it much more likely that the British Ambassador and the officials of the British Council were just not interested in the Dysteleological Surd together.

No one else was traveling with them in the car and as soon as they had moved off, Witkowski handed Hilliard an envelope.

"Inside you will find ten thousand zlotys. It is no use giving you any more as you will be unable to spend them in ten days. So we shall have to keep the rest for you until you decide to pay us another visit as the National Bank of Poland will neither give you sterling for them nor permit you to take them with you when you leave the country. If you were caught attempting to smuggle them out you would be put in prison, and even if you were successful I do not think that you would find a purchaser for them. Look!" Witkowski jabbed a forefinger at a depressing chunk of masonry sliding past the window. "Workmen's houses."

Hilliard found it difficult to pretend interest. What Witkowski had just told him was a much bigger fly in the ointment than the news that neither the British Ambassador nor the British Council was going to attend his lecture. How he was going to pay Catacomb and Priddle their commission without emptying his bank account and drawing on next month's salary he no longer had the slightest idea.

"Since the war, Warsaw has been completely rebuilt and our capital is now the same as any other big city in the world."

Witkowski was right, Hilliard thought: the grim streets through which they were now passing might have been the loveless canyons leading into Paris or Milan and the coupled red tramcars, the blistered chariots of newly liberated Vienna. Even the new broad thoroughfares in the center of the city were as devoid of glory as the boulevards of Wichita and Cincinnati. Ideology perhaps was no more than a quarrel about how to call despair hope.

"Tonight I shall leave you to rest after your journey," Witkowski said when he had helped Hilliard to register at the bleak reception desk of the Hotel Leningrad. "Of course I cannot promise that you will not be disturbed by reporters. Such, however, is the price of fame."

"Unfortunately." Hilliard did his best to look as though he were used to bearing with echelons of interviewers from *The Observer* and *The Sunday Times*.

As soon as Witkowski had gone, the reception clerk produced ten copies of *Symfonia Dysonansów* for Hilliard to autograph, one for himself and nine for his friends; the lift boy produced three and the girl in a blue uniform who kept the keys of the bedrooms on the second floor, six. Even the porter who brought up Hilliard's luggage had a copy, and the maid who put his flowers in vases beside those sent direct to the hotel by the *Polska Zjednoczona Partia Robotnicza* and the *Związek Młodzieży Socjalistycznej* another three. Left alone at last to unpack, Hilliard had just time to notice that the porter at the airport had torn Charlotte's label as well as the Polskie Linie Lotnicze tag off the handle of his suitcase when the telephone bell rang.

A press photographer, the concierge said in fair English, was waiting downstairs and would be grateful if Professor Hilliard would be kind enough to pose for him in front of the hotel.

At home it was always the wrong people who seemed to have their photographs in the papers, Hilliard thought as he walked eagerly back along the corridor to the lift. The opaque masks of the eminent, the featureless mugs of statesmen, princelings and movie stars—how well they explained the West's loss of the cold war.

The press photographer did his job thoroughly. After he had photographed Hilliard in front of the hotel, he walked him along the Marszałkowska to a bookshop window where he photographed him looking in at a display of *Symfonia Dysonansów*, and then to the Plac Defilad, where he made him pose on front of the Palac Kultury i Nauki.

When Hilliard returned to the Leningrad the concierge informed him that a reporter had arrived to interview him and was waiting in the *Kawiarnia*. The reporter insisted on Hilliard having tea and cakes with him before he began asking his questions and it was seven o'clock before Hilliard was free to go upstairs to his room.

As he bent to unlock his suitcase, he saw that both Charlotte's label and the Polskie Linie Lotnicze tag were back on the handle again.

5

It wasn't difficult for Hilliard to work out what had happened: Charlotte's label and the Polskie Linie Lotnicze tag hadn't tied themselves on to the handle again; they had never been detached from it. It was from Karminski's Revelation suitcase and not from Hilliard's that the porter at the airport had torn the label and the tag, and it was Karminski's Revelation that the porter had put into Witkowski's car for Hilliard to take to the hotel. While Hilliard had been receiving his VIP welcome, Karminski, with the porter's connivance, had made off with Hilliard's Revelation to search it. All those copies of *Symfonia Dysonansów* for autographing had been laid on by telephone from the airport to prevent Hilliard beginning to unpack before the arrival of the photographer who, like the reporter, had been sent to keep Hilliard occupied until Karminski had completed his search and replaced the suitcase.

His fears had been well-founded: the mistake about the overcoat in East Berlin coming on top of the suitcase blunder in London must have convinced Karminski and his friend that Hilliard was a spy. They must have imagined that he had provided himself with a Revelation like Karminski's and left it unlocked so as to have a plausible excuse ready if he were caught trying to open the Pole's; and his visit to the lavatory at Schönefeld they had ascribed to a desire to examine the contents of Karminski's friend's overcoat pockets in privacy.

But what could they have suspected that he had been looking for? Secret documents of some sort, Hilliard supposed. Treachery was run of the mill these days and as the holder of a diplomatic passport, Karminski could have carried as many leaked blueprints as he liked in his suitcase without fear of their being discovered by customs officials. Yet why should a security policeman—Hilliard was now certain that Karminski's friend must be at least that—who hadn't even got off the plane at London, be carrying a secret document in his overcoat pocket, and why should Karminski and the policeman have imagined that Hilliard had thought that he was?

More puzzling still, what could Karminski have hoped to find in Hilliard's suitcase? Karminski had seen that Hilliard's passport was an ordinary one and had therefore known that Hilliard had known that his suitcase had been liable to inspection by the Polish customs authorities. A camera with telescopic lens perhaps. Cameras with telescopic lenses were used for photographing military installations, Hilliard seemed to remember having read.

One thing at least was certain: however thoroughly Karminski had searched Hilliard's suitcase, he could have found nothing suspicious. Nor could he very well have expected to do so. The tumultuous welcome he had seen Hilliard receive at the airport must have persuaded him that the author of *Symfonia Dysonansów* was the last sort of person likely to be involved in sedition. His searching of Hilliard's suitcase could therefore have been little more than a routine double check and Hilliard must now be in the clear.

Nevertheless Hilliard's hands were trembling when he turned the key in the two locks. Karminski, he saw at once, had done his work so neatly that if it hadn't been for the slip up about the luggage labels he would never have known that the contents had been touched. His sponge bag, electric razor and hairbrushes, repacked by himself that morning, were still wedged clumsily down the sides. His pajamas still sprawled over Charlotte's neat layers of handkerchiefs, underclothes and shirts. The jackets were still on top of the waistcoats and the waistcoats on top of the trousers.

He tried to calm his nerves by unpacking with his usual old-maidish precision. He laid his hair brushes beside the massed flowers which made the dressing table look like a new grave and carried his electric razor and sponge bag into the bathroom. He hung each of his suits on a separate hanger in the wardrobe and put his handkerchiefs in a different drawer from his underclothes so as not to blow his nose on a pair of folded pants by mistake.

If Gomulka was not like Franco, his hoteliers seemed every bit as slaphappy. Because there was no plug on the end of the bath chain, Hilliard had to make do with a wash in the handbasin. He had run back twice into the bedroom to answer the telephone before he discovered that it was his electric razor that had made the bell ring; and as it went on clanging away like a fire engine all the time he was shaving he did not hear the knocking on his door until he had finished and disconnected the razor.

His visitor was a very young girl with a mop of red hair like a Yorkshire terrier's. She was carrying a pile of *Symfonia Dysonansów* and came rushing into the room so eagerly that she tripped. The books shot from her arms and spilled over the floor.

"There was no answer when I rang, but the concierge said he knew you must be in your room because he had seen you go up in the lift," she said in faintly accented French and nearly lost her balance again through trying to shake hands with her right hand and pick up a book with her left.

Hilliard helped her to gather up the books and explained about his razor and the telephone bell.

"I'll tell you what. I'll send down a thought to the concierge to tell him there's a faulty connection. It'll be a grand way of making a test. I'm a great believer in telepathy. Are you? Anyway the Church hasn't condemned it yet." The earnest little face was as puckered as a baked apple.

"Then you might as well send him down a thought about my bath plug while you're about it. There's none on the end of the chain and I can't wash myself properly till there is."

"Two thoughts might be too much to expect to have proved

23

at the same time. As I expect you want a bath more than you want the telephone bell stopped ringing and that'll strengthen my telepathy, I'll ring down about the telephone bell and send a thought down about the bath plug."

"I leave the choice entirely to you." She couldn't, Hilliard guessed, be more than twenty, and that was the age for bees in the bonnet.

"And while I'm telephoning perhaps you'll be kind enough to autograph these books I've brought. Your signature and the date will do for my friends but I'd be grateful if you'd put my name on my copy. It's Zamoyska: Z-A-M-O-Y-S-K-A. Wanda Zamoyska."

Miss Zamoyska had finished telephoning before Hilliard had finished signing.

"Thank you, Professor Hilliard. And now I'd like to interview you for my newspaper. *Polska Prawda*'s the name—perhaps you've heard of it. I've rather a lot of questions to ask, I'm afraid. I hope you don't mind."

"Not in the least." Although Miss Zamoyska was a reporter, Hilliard knew that she couldn't have been sent by Karminski who had already searched and replaced his suitcase. "What about your having dinner with me if you're free and that'll give us all the time in the world?" It was more than twenty years since Hilliard had dined alone with a girl and the most clairvoyant of wives could not see through an Iron Curtain.

"Thank you very much. I'd love to. I was hoping that you were going to invite me."

Hilliard found it hard to return the floor girl's smile when he handed in his key because he knew that she had been one of Karminski's accomplices in the search of his suitcase. He distrusted the liftman's servility for the same reason. A pile of *Symfonia Dysonansów* stacked under the pelmet of *L'Humanité, Sovjetunion and Chiny* above the newsstand showed him how easy it had been for them and their colleagues to procure all those copies of his book so quickly on the receipt of Karminski's telephone call from the airport. For the first

time in his life Hilliard welcomed the sound of Anglo-Saxon
voices in the lounge of a foreign hotel and was even more
reassured by Miss Zamoyska's information that the friendly
vacuous faces above the pink tickets in the lapels belonged to
members of the World Association of Matchfolder Collectors
who were holding a convention in Warsaw.

The restaurant was already crowded, but a waiter of French
extraction who Miss Zamoyska said was called Hippolyte
found them a table next to a group of Indonesian matchfolder
collectors. The Indonesian matchfolder collectors looked almost as stupid as the British and American ones and their
noisy conviviality struck Hilliard as being almost as dangerous
for world peace as hatred. A sulky blonde was sitting alone
at a table immediately beyond them, but when she caught
Hilliard's eye she smiled and beauty spread slowly up over
her assembly line face. In a darkened bar at the far end of the
restaurant an orchestra was playing and rows of bottles were
glimmering like a rood screen. A British matchfolder collector
in a striped blazer with a badge on the pocket walked up to
the blonde and asked her to dance, but the blonde shook her
head and went on ogling Hilliard so assiduously that he began
to suspect that Karminski was double-checking his double
check and had sent a Since October girl to try to inveigle him
into the revelation which the search of his suitcase had failed
to provide.

"No vodka for me, please," Miss Zamoyska said when Hippolyte had brought the menu card. "I've still got to take the
car back to the office and in Poland nobody's allowed to drive
within twenty-four hours of having touched alcohol."

But Miss Zamoyska ordered a bottle of Wodka Wyborowa
for Hilliard and translated the menu before she began ques-
tioning him:

"Professor Hilliard, in your book you argue in favour of
Creative Omnipotence. What then would you say God was
doing before He created the world?" The deadly serious face

under the scrum-half hair might have been St. Catherine of Siena's.

"God was doing nothing *before* He created the world because God, if He exists, does not do so in time and therefore there can have been neither before nor after He created the world." The blonde had disappeared. Afraid lest she had changed her table to listen in unobserved from behind and without the sound barrier of the Indonesians in between, Hilliard looked over his shoulder and saw something which startled him even more. At the very next table, less than two feet away, a small man with a boozer's pitted purple nose was scribbling ardently away in a notebook. Hilliard had been wrong about the blonde but right to be wary. Karminski hadn't given up yet. Karminski was leaving nothing to chance and had sent Purple Nose to watch Hilliard and monitor his conversation. To hide his nervousness from Miss Zamoyska, Hilliard swiped down two vodkas, one on top of the other.

"Thank you, Professor Hilliard. And now, Professor Hilliard, perhaps you would care to tell our readers about the funniest thing that has happened to you in the company of Bertrand Russell."

"I'm sorry to disappoint you, Miss Zamoyska, but nothing funny has ever happened to me in Bertrand Russell's company for the simple reason that I've never ever met the gentleman."

"Princess Margaret then, Professor Hilliard. Perhaps you would care to tell our readers about the funniest thing that has happened to you in the company of Princess Margaret."

"You've got things all wrong, I'm afraid, Miss Zamoyska. In the Western Way of Life even the most famous philosophers never meet Royalty. Matchfolder collectors perhaps—provided there don't happen to be enough bishops or jockeys about."

"The Western Way of Life then, Professor Hilliard. Perhaps you would care to tell our readers about the Western Way of Life."

"The Western Slide to Death, it ought to be called." Here surely was an infallible way of proving to Karminski and that scrivener of his at the table behind that Harold Twin-berrow Hilliard was not a British secret agent, and if what he said got under the skins of the Dysteleological Surd-scared British Ambassador and British Council officials so much the better. Teddy boys, striptease, transistors and tea-breaks, the tally of his private hates was so lengthy that they were through the *łosoś wędzony,* the *rumsztyk z rosbefu,* the melba *z owocami i ananasem* and on to the coffee and Hilliard's Koniak Ormiański before he had reached his last sentence, shouted almost at the top of his voice so that there should be no danger of Purple Nose missing it.

"And that's why I say three cheers for Burgess and Maclean."

"Thank you, Professor Hilliard. I am sure that our readers will be very interested to learn what you have just told me. But one good turn deserves another. The names of the months of the year are very poetical in Polish and if you will allow me I should like to write them down for you to show you how grateful I am for your kindness."

Unwilling to hurt her feelings by telling her that he already had a list of them in his pocket book, Hilliard let her do as she had suggested; and when she had finished the unpronounce-able syllables and their translations looked much more beauti-ful in her handwriting than in Karminski's.

Charmed by her demeanor and attracted by her expressive face, Hilliard was so sorry when she said that it was time for her to go back to the office and write up her interview that he invited her to lunch with him three days later. To his delight she accepted and he accompanied her to her car congratulating himself on having had the courage to ask her. Turning to go in again, he saw Purple Nose come rushing out of the hotel and jump into a taxi which the doorman had called for him. Convinced that Purple Nose must be on his way to tell Kar-minski that Hilliard was not a secret agent but a fellow traveler, Hilliard went back into the restaurant to celebrate.

His table was still free, but the Indonesian matchfolder collectors had gone and one of their chairs was now occupied by the blonde who switched on her eyes again as soon as she recognized Hilliard. Pretending not to notice, Hilliard scratched his Adam's apple the way he had seen Karminski do in the plane, but it was the Since October girl who answered his summons and not Hippolyte.

"Dobry wieczór Panu," she said as she sat down beside him and smoothed the folds of her white and gold dress.

"Parlez-vous français, Mademoiselle? Sprechen Sie Deutsch?"

"Tylko po Polsku." But Hippolyte was over in time to interpret the rest of what she said:

"The young lady asks me to tell Monsieur that her name is Halina and that she is very enchanted to meet Monsieur."

"Tell Mademoiselle Halina that I am enchanted to meet her." Now that he knew that it was Purple Nose and not the blonde who had been Karminski's spy, Hilliard was all set for an evening's fun.

"The young lady asks me to ask Monsieur whether Monsieur would care to dance with her."

"Tell her with pleasure. And please have a couple of Koniak Ormiański's waiting for us when we come back."

"Pamiętasz Capri i nasze spotkanie?" a violinist was crooning as Hilliard's legs were drawn into the suck of Halina's dress in the streaky gloom of the bar. Two girls in a single evening, one to dine with, one to dance with—who wanted to have funny things happen to them in the company of Bertrand Russell or Princess Margaret? "Do you remember Cap Rye and the lost time we mat?" The girls still liked Hilliard as much as Hilliard still liked the girls.

"Za noc tysiąc złotych." Halina raised her glass to Hilliard's when they were back at their table and as though warned in advance Hippolyte was there to translate:

"The lady says, Monsieur, that it's a thousand zlotys for all night."

At the Catacomb and Priddle rate of exchange a thousand zlotys worked out at roughly fifteen pounds—surely not too much to pay for eight hours with those legs that had come out all about him like scythes in the dance. In twenty-five years of marriage Hilliard had never had a night off and it would be a good way of paying back Charlotte for the embalmer at Torquay. But ought professors of philosophy who wrote about the Dysteleological Surd want to pay back? Miss Zamoyska, he was sure, would say that they ought not, and in the end it was the fear of having anything on his conscience when he met her again in three days' time which restrained him.

"Mademoiselle says that she would be grateful if Monsieur could see his way to paying her in zlotys as the cost accountants' and auctioneers' conventions have encumbered her with more dollars and sterling than she can safely unload on the black market."

"Tell her I'll take the lot—traveler's checks too if she likes." So East still met West when the policeman wasn't looking. In the long run Original Sin might turn out to be a better bet for NATO than Polaris. *Felix culpa* indeed if it paid Messrs. Catacomb and Priddle their commission! Without revealing their source, Hilliard explained that he had more zlotys than he could possibly spend during his short stay in Poland, and that he would be glad to sell them to Mademoiselle Halina for as many of the cost accountants' and auctioneers' dollars and pounds as would cover them at the black market rate of exchange.

While Hippolyte translated Hilliard calculated. His room was priced at one hundred zlotys a night, his dinner with Miss Zamoyska had cost him two hundred and twenty-five. Even allowing for a guest a meal—and he would probably be invited out for several—he couldn't spend the whole of his ten thousand zlotys in ten days. Tomorrow he would ask Witkowski for the 95,245 still due to him and say that he required them to buy a fur coat for Charlotte. Provided the black market rate of exchange wasn't too high and the Cost Accountants and Auctioneers had been generous enough, it looked as though Catacomb and Priddle's commission were in the bag. If he weren't able to insert the dollars and sterling on his foreign currency import declaration without risk of their addition being noticed he would conceal them on his person and trust to luck or his celebrity preventing his being searched by the customs authorities on his departure.

"Mademoiselle says that she is prepared to carry out both transactions with Monsieur and that the seclusion of her bedroom is as propitious for the one as for the other."

Hilliard had to think very hard about Miss Zamoyska in order to withstand the attack made by Halina's knee under the table.

"Tell her that I'm too old for anything except the exchange deal. In any case I can't give her the money tonight. Ask her if ninety-five thousand zlotys is too much for her and tell her she'll have to give me a couple of days to get hold of them." Witkowski, Hilliard was sure, wouldn't be able to produce the zloyts at less than twenty-four hours' notice.

"Mademoiselle says that if Monsieur will bring his ninety-five thousand zlotys to the Café Manekin on the Rynek Starego Miasta the day after tomorrow at eleven o'clock in the evening she will be waiting there for him with dollars and pounds to cover them at the rate of seventy zlotys to the dollar and two hundred zlotys to the pound."

"Tell her I'll be there without fail. Ask her to write down the address for me." Hilliard took Wanda's list of the Polish months from his pocket and pushed it across the table face downwards.

The British Government had made everybody accountants these days and as soon as Halina had left him to try her luck with the matchfolder collectors in the bar, Hilliard began to do sums under the address she had written out for him. £298 : 9 : 0 at 200 zlotys to the pound worked out to 59,-690 zlotys. 59,690 zlotys from 95,000 zlotys left 35,310 zlotys. 35,310 zlotys would leave him with £176 : 11 : 0 not to tell the Inland Revenue about—the British Government had made everybody cheats these days as well. He had barely put the piece of paper back into his pocket when Karminski walked up and sat down on the chair which Halina had just vacated.

"I have arrived for the drink for which you so cordially invited me. I hope that I have not responded to your kindness too soon."

"The sooner the better as far as I'm concerned." Purple Nose must have made his report by now so Karminski's visit could scarcely be other than a friendly one. Perhaps he had even come to apologize. The thought excited Hilliard into slang he hadn't used for years: "What's your tipple?"

"I shall tipple a Wiśniowka if I may. A Wiśniowka is a kind of cherry brandy. It leaves a fruity flavor in the gullet. *Wiśniowkę, prosze.*" Even when he gave his order to Hippolyte, Karminski's schoolmasterish face still looked as though it were expounding a quadratic equation. "That was a magnanimous welcome you were accorded at the airport this afternoon. I do not think that a greater assembly would have flocked to greet Sophia Monroe."

"Marilyn surely shouldn't it be?"

"Probably. These are names about which I do my best to be foggy. They stick in my throat like those of the saints—Sophia Monroe, Margaret Marilyn Alacoque, they are merely different brands of opium for the people."

"For my part I prefer the Alacoques." Hilliard saw now that Karminski's mistake had been deliberate.

"And I prefer the Lollobardots: they at least are still alive and can be conditioned. Even famous professors of philosophy can be conditioned sometimes." The smile that passed across the wintry face scarcely creased the corners of the thin lips. "Why did you not tell me in the plane that you were so well-known in Poland? Was it because you did not wish to blow your own trumpet?" Not content with having sent Purple Nose to watch Hilliard at dinner and listen in to his conversation, Karminski had obviously been checking up on his own.

"There didn't seem to me to be any special necessity."

"But at home too you do not blush unseen? Your name appears in *Who's Who*?"

"In America it does." Only three Americans out of every ten thousand had their names in *Who's Who in America*, the editors said. If Hilliard was a nobody in Great Britain, in the United States he was a man in three thousand three hundred and thirty-three recurring.

Karminski nodded without saying anything. His attention now seemed to be concentrated on the entrance and when Hilliard turned round he saw why. Blocking the doorway was the burly body of Admiral Sir David Doddick. The Admiral had hoisted his new flag, the pink lapel ticket of the Match-folder Collectors' Convention, and his eyes were sweeping over all the tables in the restaurant like searchlights. At the last the beam fell on the shoal of silver shoes gleaming in the bar and he came charging down past Hilliard and Karminski like an Ionescu rhinoceros flaring a television set.

"There is going to be dirty work at the crossroads," Karminski said.

"Boys will be boys."

"That is not what I meant. I meant that I do not think that the Admiral has come from his meeting with the General de Gaulle in Paris merely in order to attend the Matchfolders' Convention in Warsaw."

"Why on earth not? Matchfolder collecting's just the hobby to appeal to a retired naval numskull." Although he preferred that Karminski should take the Admiral for a secret agent rather than himself, Hilliard was much too irritated by Karminski's suspiciousness to let it go unchallenged.

"I do not think that the Admiral is a retired naval numskull. I think that the Admiral is still an active naval numskull. Nor do I think that it is only matchfolders which he collects." Karminski pointed down to the bar where the Admiral could already be seen revolving with Halina's white and gold dress. "Sticking to his hulk like a barnacle, would you not say?"

"It's all in character. Only old men cretinous enough to 'belie their soul's immensity' by collecting matchfolders can imagine that girls young enough to be their granddaughters can have anything but a financial interest in their decrepitude. As Marcel Proust puts it so pungently, elderly lovers always forget that lust only makes their ugly mugs uglier still in the eyes of the pretty girls they are panting to get into bed with."

"That is very true. Let us hope then that the Admiral Tomato will have learned by heart the long sausages of wisdom of Marcel Proust. *Hop siup!* Down the hatch!" Karminski emptied at a gulp the glass of sticky red liqueur which Hippolyte had brought him. "I do not wish to interfere with any arrangements which may have been made for you, but the church of Our Lady in Kraków is well worth a visit and you should on no account miss seeing its stately spire."

"I expect that Witkowski will already have laid that on for me." Hilliard didn't want there to be any risk of Karminski offering to be his guide: being shown round a church by Karminski would be rather like going to Lourdes on a pilgrimage conducted by John Osborne.

"No doubt." After a long silent stare Karminski rose abruptly, shooting out fingers as stiff as glove stretchers. "Goodnight, Professor Hilliard. I thank you for the hospitable drink and I wish you pleasant dreams."

When Hilliard went up to bed he found a man arguing heatedly with the floor girl at her desk. As he approached to ask for his key the man turned round to display a pitted purple nose and, in the lapel of his jacket which Hilliard hadn't been able to see in the dining room, the pink ticket of the Matchfolder Collectors' Convention.

"See here, Mister," Purple Nose said to Hilliard, "Ah canna get this lassie to understand one word Ah'm saying. Tell her that if she thinks Ah'm paying fifteen zlotys for having a shirt washed she's mistaken. Ah've been working it out in this wee book here: four and elevenpence is what it comes to and not a penny less." The notebook which Purple Nose held out for Hilliard's inspection was the one Hilliard had seen him scribbling in in the dining room.

"Sixty-seven zlotys to the pound is an artificial rate, that's what you've got to remember. At the black market rate you'd probably find out that it didn't work out so badly." Hilliard was talking so as not to have to think and would probably have gone on to explain about the National Bank of Poland's need to build up foreign currency reserves as cheaply as possible had he not suddenly realized that if Karminski really did still suspect him of being a spy he would make a point of reading tomorrow's *Polska Prawda* and would learn then what Hilliard had said to Miss Zamoyska about the Western Slide to Death. At the very worst therefore the effects of his strategy had only been postponed.

"Tell the lassie, Ah'm asking ye. Tell her that Ah'm no paying fifteen zlotys for having a shirt washed. Tell her that if she canna do better than that Ah'll send them to an outside laundry as sure as ma name's Hector MacOgg."

"Monsieur me charge de vous dire qu'il trouve un peu cher votre prix de quinze zlotys pour laver une chemise et que si vous ne pouvez pas lui accorder un escompte il se trouvera dans l'obligation de s'adresser à une blanchisserie du dehors aussi sûrement qu'il s'appelle Hector MacOgg."

"Man, ye've got a grand grip of the Polish, Ah can see that. And now what's the lassie got to say for herself?"

"The lassie says that a discount's out of the question. The lassie says that if Mr. Gomulka or Cardinal Wyszynski stayed here they'd be required to pay fifteen zlotys for having their shirts washed the same as Mr. Hector MacOgg."

A matchfolder's transistor was moaning masturbatorily through the wall when Hilliard at last reached his room. While plugging his ears with the wax pellets which he always carried as protection against the decibels of progress, he noticed that his briefcase was propped more obliquely against the chair than when he had gone down to dinner with Miss Zamoyska. Opening it, he found that the mnemonic summary of his lecture which he had clipped to the top of the manuscript was now clipped underneath.

Pottering over undressing wasn't Hilliard's only disobedience to Charlotte that night; instead of pulling his socks right way round again before he got into bed he left them lying on the floor inside out.

6

Next morning Hilliard awoke late from a troubled sleep. Pale sunlight lay sparkling on the black carpet like puddles of Pilsener. When he pulled back the curtain a block of Orwellian looking office buildings opposite suggested ten floors of typists pounding out yet another exegesis of Karl Marx. From the pavement below however came a reassuring shout of *"Merde!"*: French culture had sent its representative to the Matchfolder Collectors' Convention.

Both Miss Zamoyska's telepathy and telephoning had been unsuccessful: there was still no plug on the end of the bath chain and the telephone bell in the bedroom rang the whole time Hilliard was shaving. As he finished dressing there was a knock on the door. When Hilliard opened it a sandy haired little man bounded in, waited until Hilliard had closed the door again and then said with a grin:

"I do not wish to interfere with any arrangements which may have been made for you, but the church of Our Lady in Kraków is well worth a visit and you should on no account miss seeing its stately spire. All right. Let's cut out the versicles, shall we? I realized you were Whale as soon as I read about you in last night's newspapers. Caviare said they were sending out a literary gent this time. How is he by the bye? Wood from the neck up as usual, I suppose?" Putting his fingers to his lips as a second knock sounded outside, the little man dived into the bathroom and pulled the door to behind him.

To Hilliard's consternation his new visitor was Karminski.

"Just the very chap I wanted to see," Hilliard said as jovially as he could. "After you left last night I ran into a Scottish matchfolder collector. He was kicking up hell because the hotel people wanted to charge him fifteen zlotys for washing a shirt. What would *you* say was a fair price?"

"My wife always washes my shirts for me so I would not know."

Hilliard steered Karminski quickly past the closed bathroom door. Had Karminski been trailing the little man? If he had and had seen him entering, Hilliard was sunk. For the little man was obviously a real British agent who had made the same error as Karminski and taken Hilliard for another British agent apparently called Whale. Some as yet undetected fellow traveler in M.I.5 must have told Karminski about this Whale and provided him with the password which he had tried out on Hilliard in the restaurant last night. And it was Hilliard's secondary profession as a writer even more than his blunders about the suitcase and the overcoat which had made Karminski and his policeman friend imagine that he was the literary spy they had obviously been sent over to London from Warsaw to trail.

When he had folded his long body in three sequences of right angles into the only armchair in the room, Karminski pulled a newspaper out of his overcoat pocket and held it up to display the name POLSKA PRAWDA.

"Just what am I to understand by this letting down of the side, Professor Hilliard?"

"Letting down my hair would perhaps be a more correct term." Hilliard's panic began to subside: not only had Karminski not seen the little man entering Hilliard's room, but he was swallowing the bait. "And I can't tell you how glad I was to have the opportunity. We professors have to watch our step on the home ground."

Karminski looked at Hilliard for a long time in silence before saying anything.

"In other words, Professor Hilliard, you wish me to understand that you have been converted to our way of thinking?"

"That's one way of putting it, but I'm not so sure that it's the correct one. There was no sudden light on the way to Damascus. Like most British intellectuals my sympathies have always been with the Left."

"Even so it was imprudent to communicate those views of yours to a newspaper reporter. The proper procedure surely was to tell me quietly about them on the plane. Things would then have been much easier for us both. I am however the last person to look a gift horse in the face, especially when it is not only the horse that is a gift but also the load that the horse carries. Professor Hilliard, just who and where is the British agent who works in Poland and who is known as Sardine?"

Sardine, Whale, Caviare—obviously the whole network had the names of fish and it must be Sardine who was hiding in the bathroom. Hilliard now saw that he had been too clever by half and that, far from extricating himself from a precarious situation, he had put himself in one very much more perilous: instead of convincing Karminski that he was not a British agent, his denunciation of the Western Way of Life had made Karminski think that he was a British agent who wanted to change sides and work for the East. Whatever his country's failings, Hilliard wasn't going to purchase his safety by betraying one of its servants whose face he had rather liked. On the eighth of September 1940, even the Royal Army Pay Corps had been called out to defend the island fortress in Edinburgh and 462739445837 Private Hilliard, H.T., had been issued with a revolver he hadn't known how to fire and ordered to repulse all German tanks advancing up Leith Walk. A return of the same sort of bravado enabled him to see that his only defence now was attack:

"Why do you people always make the stupid mistake of imagining that we are as crooked as you are? I am no more a spy than the poor Admiral is. What I said to *Polska Prawda* was an expression of opinion, that's all—nothing more is to be read into it than into the interview I gave that reporter you sent to keep me out of my room while you were changing the suitcases round again."

"So you spotted my guile, did you?" Karminski's grin was shameless.

"Only because of the stupidity of the porter at the airport. He left both my luggage labels on and tore both yours off."

"In that case I must give him a raspberry."

"The rest was perfect, the books you laid on for me to sign, the photographer, everything."

"I am glad that you were impressed. It may teach you to cover up your tracks more carefully the next time you want to pry into suitcases and overcoat pockets."

"Surely that's a proof of my innocence—a real spy would never have been as clumsy as I was." In the end only trams had come up Leith Walk on the eighth of September 1940 and Private Hilliard, H.T., hadn't been required to fire the revolver he hadn't known how to. This time however the alarm seemed unlikely to turn out a false one. "Let's get things straight, Mr. Karminski. I am not, repeat, not this person you seem to be looking for and I have never, repeat, never heard of this other person called Sardine."

"If you are not, repeat, not the person I am looking for and if you have never, repeat, never heard of this other person called Sardine how does it happen that you are familiar with the Hush-hush way of sending signals?"

"The Rush-rush sent signals too: 'B Company Acquittance Rolls not, repeat, not received stop. Please forward immediately, repeat, immediately stop.'"

"Naturally, Professor Hilliard, it does not surprise me that in the sober light of dawn you should have second thoughts. But *your* second thoughts will not change *my* first thoughts which are that you are a British agent called Whale sent to Poland to contact another British agent called Sardine. What cover story could be more likely to obtain a visa from our Polish Consulate in London than the true cover story of a professor who has written a Polish best seller and who has been invited to lecture to the Towarzystwo Metafizyczne w Warszawie? You come to Warsaw, you are greeted at the airport

38

with clamorous acclaim, you deliver your spout, you give Sardine his latest terms of reference and you beetle back to England without having aroused a breath of suspicion. It is as easy as falling off a log."

"Unfortunately for your argument, your major premise is wrong. All true stories are not true *cover* stories."

"If it is a question of price the sky is the limit, but we cannot talk about that until we are sure that your indiscretions to *Polska Prawda* have not been reported in the British press and made it impossible for us to employ you in England."

"Once and for all, Mr. Karminski, you're barking up the wrong tree. I am not this person you say is called Whale and I haven't the slightest knowledge of this other person you say is called Sardine. The reason I griped to *Polska Prawda* the way I did was to get my own back on the British Ambassador and the British Council for having thought up phony excuses for not attending my lecture to the Towarzystwo Metafizyczne w Warszawie tonight."

"That is not what you said a few minutes ago. The tale you spun me a few minutes ago was that it was a relief to be able to express to *Polska Prawda* the opinions you hadn't been able to get off your chest at home because of your position as a university professor. And how is it that when you do not know a word of Polish you are able to pronounce Towarzystwo Metafizyczne w Warszawie correctly?"

"I can also say *'Panie i panowie'* for 'Ladies and gentlemen' but that doesn't mean I speak Polish. And if you don't believe what I told you about the British Ambassador and British Council it oughtn't to be so difficult for you to check. The reason they both said they couldn't come to my lecture was because they were going to spend a few days in the country."

"Naturally, Professor Hilliard, I can understand you wanting to think the matter over before you commit yourself, and so for the moment I shall refrain from turning on the heat."

"Turning on the heat can't make me a person I'm not." But Hilliard took care not to say this too defiantly: it was beginning

39

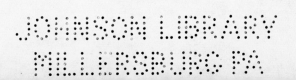

to dawn on him that the revolver he didn't know how to fire might be made to stop the German tanks after all. Karminski had spoken about employing him in England if his interview with *Polska Prawda* were not reported in the British press. In order to employ him in England, Karminski would have to allow him to return to England. Once back in England he would do a doublecross: instead of telling Karminski about M.I.5, Hilliard would tell M.I.5 about Karminski and the fellow traveler still in their midst and be rewarded with an O.B.E. or an invitation to a Garden Party. The only snag was Sardine. But if Hilliard admitted that he was Whale perhaps Karminski would believe him when he said that Sardine hadn't kept his rendezvous and conclude that Sardine had got cold feet and gone to ground. In the meantime Karminski would probably find it natural that Hilliard should play for safety and not own up to being Whale until Karminski made him a definite offer. "Of course what you choose to believe about me is you own affair, Mr. Karminski. Cardinal Newman said that you could neither argue a man into conviction or out of it."

"I did not know that a Cardinal could be so down to earth. Our Cardinal here in Poland is up in the clouds."

When the bang came from the bathroom Hilliard didn't follow Karminski as he darted along the passage. He sat where he was on the bed and aspired that for once God would abrogate effect and save His child Harold from being sucked under by the Dysteleological Surd. He heard voices in Polish. The one he thought he recognized as Karminski's sounded angry and there was a scowl on Karminski's face when he came striding back.

"You ought to have warned me about that plumber, Professor Hilliard. How do you know he doesn't understand English?"

"I'm sorry, but the idea never struck me." Hilliard's relief was so great that he was afraid Karminski would see it flashing about his brain like a goldfish in a bowl. "Anyway the bath-

40

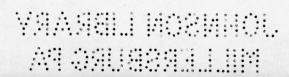

room door was shut so I don't suppose he could have heard what we were saying."

"And how does it happen that you were able to tell the maid that there was no plug in your bath when the only words you know in Polish are Towarzystwo Metafizyczne w Warszawie and *panie i panowie*?"

"I didn't tell anybody. The maid must have noticed for herself that the plug was missing." Wood from the neck up? Caviare could scarcely be that to have chosen an agent as astute as Sardine. And how fortunate it was that Miss Zamoyska's telepathy should have had as little effect as her telephoning.

"Anyway from now on you will be able to enjoy your tub. All right, Professor Hilliard, for the moment I shall leave you, but if a nod is as good as a wink to a blind horse let me warn you that the penalty in this country for espionage is death."

"Careless of me to have knocked over that stool," Sardine said with a grin when he came out of the bathroom. "If I hadn't noticed that missing bath plug in time we'd both of us have been done for. In case you don't know, that was *Bekas*—Snipe in English and as cunning as they come. For all I know he may only have been pretending to believe me about the bath plug so I'd better beat it in case he comes sneaking back. Eleven hundred hours the day after tomorrow at the gates of the Powązki military cemetery—I'll give you all the dirt then."

After breakfast in the *Kawiarnia* surrounded by American matchfolder collectors clamoring for waffles, Hilliard went for a walk along the Marszałkowska to clear his brain. When he reached the Aleje Jerozolimskie, all six of his bracer clips were still holding. This, and the sight on his return of a bootblack who looked like Piłsudski reading *Symfonia Dysonansów* in the front hall of the hotel, he tried to interpret as good omens.

7

Witkowski obviously didn't believe the story about Charlotte and the fur coat when Hilliard told him at lunch that he wanted the balance of his royalties paid over in cash next morning. The publisher's taciturnity after he had seen the wink Halina gave Hilliard on her way down to the bar made it clear just how he thought Hilliard was going to spend the ninety-five thousand zlotys.

But Hilliard had too much else on his mind to worry about Witkowski's suspicions. Although to the best of his knowledge he had not been followed on his walk along the Marszałkowska he knew that it was quite possible that he had. If Karminski were having him trailed and learned that he met a man at the gates of the Powązki military cemetery Hilliard would never be able to make Karminski believe that he had been unable to contact Sardine and the whole of his plan would fall through. Oughtn't he therefore to play for safety and take the first plane home after he had given his lecture and let the £298 : 9 : 0 to pay Catacomb and Priddle's commission and the £176 : 11 : 0 not to tell the Inland Revenue about go hang? But would he in fact be able to take a plane home? Wouldn't Karminski have given orders to the officials at the airport that the famous Professor Hilliard was not to be allowed to leave the country? Wasn't the only course now left open to him not to turn up at the cemetery, trust that Sardine would smell a rat and not risk coming back to the hotel to see him, exchange his zlotys into pounds and dollars with Halina and hope that his interview with *Polska Prawda* had escaped the notice of the British press? Inspired by self-interest, fear, acceptance of the inevitable, Wodka Wyborowa and Koniak Ormiański, Hilliard decided that it was.

But the few drinks he had been able to have beforehand weren't much help to him when he faced the members of the Towarzystwo Metafizyczne w Warszawie at eight o'clock in the Palac Kultury i Nauki. The salt of the earth in Warsaw like the salt of the earth in London or Aberdeen resembled a gathering of unsuccessful railway booking clerks. One of the mysteries which no metaphysic had ever been able to resolve was why well-dressed morons should have the confident bearing of encyclopedists and encyclopedists the humble demeanor of morons. Miss Zamoyska's tousled hair wasn't anywhere to be seen among the gloomy faces at the press table and the only bright feature was the absence of Karminski whose chilly head Hilliard had half-expected to see among the beards and udders in the front row.

Hilliard was so nervous that he was afraid to trust to his memory and for the first time in his life read his lecture word for word from the manuscript. After every four or five sentences he paused for Witkowski to translate them into Polish. It was while Witkowski was translating Geddes MacGregor's exposition of the Dysteleological Surd that Hilliard's first bracer clip gave, and while Hilliard himself was quoting Kant's refutation of Anselm's ontology, the second.

As the other four clips were still holding when he got back to the Leningrad, he made a dash towards the bar for the alcohol with which his hosts had failed to provide him. Charging through the restaurant, he was stopped by MacOgg who was sitting at a table with Admiral Sir David Doddick.

"Ah've been telling His Nibs here about the downright outrageous price this hotel asks for washing shirts, but he's nae mair help than you were. No offence meant of course, so ye might as well sit down and jine us. Ye make me feel that giddy towering away up there like the Walter Scott monument."

"You in the matchfolder racket too?" the Admiral asked as

Hilliard reluctantly pulled out a chair. Hilliard saw at once that the Admiral had no recollection of their previous meeting in the Athenaeum.

"No; I'm over here on business." It was the white lie Hilliard always told when he traveled: strangers, he had generally found, were embarrassed by the mention of erudition.

"What's yours, Arbuthnot? I'd better ask you because Mac-Oggski won't."

Hilliard didn't like being called Arbuthnot and found the tipsy banter between the Admiral and MacOgg boring. As soon as he could, he asked to be excused and rose with such alacrity that his four bracer clips which were still holding sprang loose simultaneously.

"My braces," he explained as he clutched at his trousers. "These new fangled clip contraptions are no use at all."

"You're right there," MacOgg said. "Ah'd rather keep ma breeks up with string any day of the week."

"Stolen from Polish laundry parcels for preference, that right, MacOggski? But even if the worst comes to the worst, Arbuthnot, I shouldn't worry too much: as far as most of these young women are concerned I expect it's all rather *déjà vu*."

"The lavatory, please," Hilliard said as he hobbled across to Hippolyte with both hands in his pockets, and the waiter led Hilliard along a passage to two doors labeled MĘSKI and DAMSKI.

Such for most people was the only essential literature, Hilliard thought as he went in to fasten his braces in the *męski*.

8

Witkowski came to the hotel next afternoon and paid Hilliard the 95,245 zlotys in his bedroom. Except for the two hundred and forty-five the money was all in five-hundred-zloty notes. One hundred and ninety of them however were more than Hilliard could carry in his wallet and when he set out for the Rynek Starego Miasta at half past ten, both his jacket and his trouser pockets were bulging.

Hippolyte hadn't been on duty in the restaurant that evening and Hilliard was frightened to ask the doorman to call a taxi for fear that he might have been suborned by Karminski. Pretending that he was going for a stroll, he crossed over to the other side of the Marszałkowska and as soon as he was sure he wasn't being followed doubled back to the taxi rank. Jumping into the first cab he came to, he showed the driver the address Halina had written down for him on the back of Miss Zamoyska's list of the Polish months.

The taxi made off in the opposite direction to that which Hilliard had taken for his walk the previous morning. Although there were fewer of them, the neon signs were as brash as those on Lexington Avenue but the lighted trams were incandescent with glory. At the end of the Marszałkowska the taxi turned sharp right and ran along the edge of a blotted out park. When Hilliard looked through the window at the back of the cab he was glad to see that there were no other car lamps boring through the darkness behind.

The Rynek Starego Miasta lay in the same gentle prayerful glow as the Place des Vosges in Paris, and Hilliard was amazed by the authenticity of its reconstructed medieval buildings. He gave the driver thirty zlotys and as soon as he saw that the man wasn't going to grumble, ran into the lighted entrance of the Manekin. A noise of voices told him that the café must be downstairs and he was searching a fog of to-bacco smoke in the basement for a glint of golden hair when he heard himself hailed by Admiral Sir David Doddick:

"Arbuthnot! Come and have one on Caledonia Stern and Wild!"

With the Admiral and MacOgg was Halina who was wear-ing the white and gold dress Hilliard had seen her in two nights ago. The encounter was awkward because Hilliard had relied on his exchange deal taking place without witnesses. He knew that this must have been Halina's expectation too when she put her finger to her lips and shook her head vig-orously while the Admiral and MacOgg were greeting him.

"Would you believe it?" The Admiral pointed at a pale blue linen bag lying under the table. "MacOggski's been trailing those shirts of his round the whole of Warsaw looking for a laundry that'll wash 'em for ten zlotys. And what's more I'm not so sure that he didn't bring some dirty ones with him from Scotland so that he could speculate against the pound by trying to get them washed cheaper behind the Iron Curtain than in Kirriemuir. Drawers too I expect if the whole revolt-ing truth were known."

"Kirkcaldy, no Kirriemuir. And it so happens Ah dinna wear drawers—they tickle ma legs."

"I'm ashamed of you, MacOggski—trying to whet an in-nocent young girl's appetite like that. And now if you don't see any objection, I'm going to order that drink you so kindly promised Arbuthnot."

"Order away. Order every dashed thing in the house. Ah'm no mean, if that's what you're trying to insinuate."

But even after his fourth cognac, Hilliard was still far from having caught up with the Admiral and MacOgg whose im-patience with each other was rapidly degenerating into a quarrel.

"What do ye want to go and call on the Ambassador at this time of night for, I'd like to know."

"Because dear old Nodder's got some kind of jollification on this evening and I promised the old boy I'd look in." Hilliard was now more convinced than ever that his interpretation of the Ambassador's non-attendance at his lecture had been correct: if His Excellency had not been deliberately avoiding the Dysteleological Surd, his visit to the country must have been a remarkably short one.

"Dah old Noddah!" MacOgg's imitation of the Admiral was so accurate that Hilliard wondered why MacOgg didn't talk like the Admiral all the time instead of like MacOgg all the time. "And what's Lady Noddah call herself—Bluebell?"

"Come on, Arbuthnot." The Admiral rose unsteadily to his feet. "Let's leave the uncouth MacOggski to his little bit of stuffski. Nodder will be delighted to make your acquaintance, I'm sure."

"Uncouth, am Ah? And what's running away and leaving me to pay for all yon drinks, might Ah ask?"

"The Sassenachs are going to pay for your drinks, MacOggski. The Sassenachs are going to pay for the potations of the Pict. Five hundred each ought to do it, I'd say, Arbuthnot."

Hilliard detached a brown note from a wad and handed it to the Admiral. The cost of MacOgg's drinks would be a cheap price to pay for being left alone with Halina, and Hilliard had thought out a plan.

"You're the chap who ought to be going with the Admiral, Mr. MacOgg," he said. "If there's anybody who knows where to get a shirt washed in Warsaw for ten zlotys it'll be the British Ambassador."

"The credit squeeze, ye mean?" For a few seconds the Scotsman's arrogant eyes shone with cupidity and then glazed over again. "Ah'm biding here wi' the lassie. In any case His Nibs is the proper person to ask dah old Noddah. Ah'm much too uncouth."

While the Admiral was paying the waiter, Hilliard made desperate signs at Halina, but she merely blew him a kiss and said: *"Jutro!"*

"Tomorrow, Arbuthnot, that's what she's saying," the Admiral said as he pocketed the change from the two five hundred zloty notes. "Probably she wants to find out if your legs are as allergic to drawers as MacOggski's so we'd better ask Nodder if he can fit you out with one of those suits of armour he ought to have standing about his baronial halls. What's the matter now, MacOggski? Don't tell me you want us to cough up for *l'amour* as well."

"Ma bag! Ye're forgetting ma bag. Ye heard what Mr. Thingummy here said, didn't ye? Well, what for do ye no take ma bag with ye and ask dah old Noddah if he doesna ken a laundry that washes shirts for ten zlotys? Or are ye feared he'll think ye uncouth?"

"What you really mean, MacOggski, don't you? is that *you* fear that having to carry your laundry bag yourself may impede the gestures of affection you foresee you are going to feel prompted to make to your lady friend before the evening's out. Come on, Arbuthnot. Charity beareth all things, even laundry bags."

But it was Hilliard who had to carry the laundry bag so that the Admiral could have the use of both arms to heave himself up the narrow stairway. There were no taxis on the Rynek Starego Miasta and they had to walk to the Krakowskie Przedmieście before a driver answered the Admiral's bellowing.

From behind the golden windows of the British Embassy came the measured dirge of official jubilation.

"The bun fight's still on," the Admiral said as he took over the laundry bag to make it easier for Hilliard to pay the taxi driver.

In the front hall was the Ambassador himself, marked out with silver braid like a tennis court.

"Timeo Danaos et dona ferentes, Tomato, old boy." The

Ambassador popped a discreetly avaricious eye at the laundry bag. "What'll be there to meet my gaze when I open to see what Sinbad has brought me? Oranges, I hope—H.M.G.'s little drops of gin could do with some protective coloring."

"Shirts from Kirkcaldy, Nodder old boy, landed on me by an inconsiderate Scottish matchfolder collector. Sorry to have made your mouth water." As the Admiral tossed the laundry bag to the cloakroom attendant, Hilliard realized that the Admiral had never had any intention of carrying out MacOgg's commission and asking the Ambassador where one could have a shirt washed in Warsaw for less than fifteen zlotys. "And now allow me to introduce my friend, Arbuthnot, over here to help the export drive. Tractors or television sets, is it, Arbuthnot? You never told me."

"How d'ye do?" The Ambassador stared glassily at Hilliard as though he were a bus he didn't want to board or an advertisement for ketchup, and when they reached the top of the staircase he was still talking exclusively to the Admiral. "Look, Tomato, there's a favor you could do me if you wouldn't mind. Since the coexistence squabble between Khrushchev and Mao, Gomulka's ordered all the other bumsucks to boycott Cathay, so if you'd paddle across and have a natter with Hoo Flung Dung over there I'd be grateful." The Ambassador nodded in the direction of a decked out Chinaman standing all alone on the far side of the room.

"Of course, old boy. Anything to oblige." The Admiral lurched away so navally that all the festooned female behinds near him seemed to bob up and down like lifebuoys. Hilliard was left alone with the Ambassador's starchy face.

"Although I've never gone in for matchfolder collecting myself, Mr.—Arbuthnot, as an indoor sport for rainy climates it probably has its points. Poland has a rainy climate, Mr.—Arbuthnot. Eight hundred to fifteen hundred millimeters of precipitation in the Carpathians and the Sudetics, Mr.—Arbuthnot. No doubt that's why the matchfolder collectors chose to hold their convention in Warsaw this year, Mr.—Arbuth-not."

The constant repetition of the absurd vocative and the deliberate pause each time before it was pronounced made Hilliard realize that the Ambassador, like Karminski and Sardine, had mistaken him for Whale about whose mission in Warsaw His Excellency had no doubt been tipped off unofficially. But, as tractors had as little to do with literature as had television, the Ambassador couldn't have been informed about the nature of Whale's cover story and must have based his deduction on Hilliard's unease when the Admiral had introduced him by a name which was not his own.

"A little vodka, Mr.—Arbuthnot? Or perhaps brandy would be more to your taste?" Hilliard would never have known that the flunky with the tray of glasses was an extra, if perched on top of the brown velvet there hadn't been Hippolyte's mournful face, which however discreetly gave no sign of recognition.

"Voyons donc, Excellence!" The affected French came sailing across from a middle aged woman glittering like a cinema entrance, and from the wan smile she gave the Ambassador when her bleak eye caught his, Hilliard guessed that she must be Bluebell.

"Fellow called Hilliard seems to have been letting the side down, Mr.—Arbuthnot. Been talking sedition to a paper called *Polska Prawda*—our sedition, not theirs. Apparently he's a professor of physiology or something at one of those lavatory tile universities where they turn out Communists and he's over here to lecture on the Dynamic Turd or something or other. I was wondering if you mightn't have run into him in your hotel by any chance, Mr.—Arbuthnot."

"Not that I'm aware of, your Excellency." In view of this development, Hilliard thought that it was safer that the Ambassador should go on imagining that he was Whale *alias* Arbuthnot than discover that he was Arbuthnot *alias* Hilliard.

"Anyway if you see a chap with long hair and a dirty neck

50

sneaking along a corridor as though he were on the prowl for a good-looking sardine to entangle in the fate worse than death, that's the chap for you to sandbag, Mr.—Arbuthnot." The hint behind the Ambassador's sketchy smile showed through like the watermark on a banknote held up to the light by a distrustful cashier. "Anyway, thank God I wasn't fool enough to let myself in for the fellow's lecture on the Dynamic Turd. *Amusez-vous bien, Monsieur—Arbuthnot!*" The Ambassador nodded curtly and walked away towards a new outbreak of music in the adjoining ballroom.

The Admiral and the Chinese Ambassador were nowhere to be seen, so Hilliard derived what companionship he could from listening in to the pontifical imbecilities uttered by those around him—Proust apparently had been read with as little profit as St. Paul. When at last he felt somebody glide up behind him it wasn't a plenipotentiary anxious to discuss the Common Market or polo, but Hippolyte back with his trayful of glasses.

"Monsieur is perhaps surprised to see me in these surroundings, but needs must when the devil drives: the Leningrad doesn't pay much and the matchfolder collectors tip even less generously than the cost accountants and the auctioneers. Monsieur, if I may say so, is looking sad. I trust that it is not because there has been a hitch in his deal this evening with Mademoiselle Halina at the Café Manekin."

"A hitch is the word. The man you may have seen me arrive with and another matchfolder collector were with her when I got there and the other matchfolder collector refused to come unstuck. All I could get out of her was something about tomorrow, but although she didn't say where or when I expect she meant the Manekin again at eleven o'clock."

"That I shall make it my business to ascertain for Monsieur. In the meantime if Monsieur is looking for the friend with whom he arrived I am sorry to have to tell Monsieur that he departed half an hour ago in the company of His Excellency the Chinese Ambassador."

Already, Hilliard saw when he looked round, the careful faces were beginning to thin out. Without bothering to look for the Ambassador to say goodby to him, Hilliard slunk downstairs and managed to make the cloakroom attendant understand that he wanted his hat and coat and a taxi. Only when he was undressing in his room at the Leningrad did he realize that he had forgotten to ask for MacOgg's laundry bag and wondered if the Admiral had remembered to do so, but was still feeling too resentful against the Scot to care.

9

Hilliard was awakened next morning by thumping on his door. His visitor was again Karminski who strode in with his hands held motionlessly by his sides and folded himself down on top of Hilliard's underclothes on the armchair.

"Professor Hilliard, in the bus on the way to London airport you informed me that you did not know Admiral Sir David Doddick. Now I find that you are very well acquainted with him indeed. Why did you tell me this packet of lies?"

"It wasn't a packet of lies. It was a packet of truth. I didn't know the Admiral then. But the other night that Scottish matchfolder collector I was telling you about who was too mean to pay fifteen zlotys for having his shirts washed introduced me." Whether Karminski had had Hilliard followed on his walk along the Marszałkowska or not he had obviously been having him watched in the Leningrad.

"How do I know that it wasn't the Admiral who was too mean to pay fifteen zlotys for having his shirts washed and that it was not he who introduced you to the Scottish matchfolder collector?"

"Have a heart, Mr. Karminski. Britain no longer rules the waves, I know, but her retired Admirals can still afford to pay fifteen zlotys for having their shirts washed." The vodka Hilliard had drunk since his arrival in Warsaw was beginning to make his belly swell out through the vent in his pajama trousers, but it was as much to give an impression of unconcern as to hide his hairiness that he slid back into bed and pulled up the sheets.

"Shall I tell you what I think, Professor Hilliard? I think

that the Admiral was only pretending not to know you when he passed by our table two nights ago in the restaurant and that you were only pretending not to know the Admiral. I think that just as you are here for a purpose which has nothing to do with the Towarzystwo Metafizyczne w Warszawie so the Admiral is here for a purpose which has nothing to do with the Matchfolder Collectors' Convention."

"Shall I tell you what *I* think, Mr. Karminski? I think that with an imagination like yours you ought to have been a novelist." It was a feeble reply, Hilliard knew, but he doubted whether the real Whale could have given a better at such short notice.

"Imagination is useful in *our* profession, Professor Hilliard, especially when it is substantiated by facts. The first fact that I know about you and the Admiral is that you drank with him here in this hotel after your lecture to the Towarzystwo Metafizyczne."

"That was when the Scotsman introduced me. I was on my way through the restaurant to the bar when this fellow Mac-Ogg buttonholed me and for politeness's sake I had to sit down and join them."

"And the second fact that I know about you and the Admiral is that last night you attended a reception at the British Embassy in his company. If it was the Scotsman who introduced you to the Admiral why was it not the Scotsman instead of yourself whom the Admiral took with him to this function?"

"Because the Scotsman had a previous engagement." Hilliard wasn't going to mention Halina or the Manekin if he could help it: if, as was likely, Karminski's informant had been an employee or a satellite guest at the British Embassy, it was only about his presence at the reception that Karminski would know, and as Hilliard still had his exchange deal to carry through he didn't want there to be any risk of a snooper being sent to the Rynek Starego Miasta that evening.

"If the Scotsman was unable to accompany the Admiral

to the reception why could not the Admiral have attended it alone? Why did he have to invite you whom you ask me believe that he had met for the first time in his life only the evening before?"

"He said that it was because he wanted to introduce me to the British Ambassador but I think the real reason was because he wanted somebody to carry MacOgg's dirty shirts for him. This MacOgg's a practical sort of fellow, you see, and he thought that if anyone in Warsaw was likely to know where you could get a shirt washed in Warsaw for less than fifteen zlotys it would be the British Ambassador."

"Tell that to the Royal Marines! The Admiral surely could have obtained that information from the Ambassador without having to take the shirts with him."

"I've already told you that MacOgg's a realist, haven't I? Probably he thought he stood a better chance of getting his shirts washed for less than fifteen zlotys if they were sent out with the rest of the embassy linen and got the benefit of a wholesale price. Anyway that's the way it was." Karminski's informer, whoever he was, couldn't have been the cloakroom attendant otherwise Karminski would have known about the laundry bag.

"Even so this brotherly act of carrying the shirts to protect the Admiral's dignity doesn't explain why the Admiral should have introduced you to the British Ambassador as Mr. Arbuthnot instead of as Professor Hilliard."

"Arbuthnot's like George. It's a name one gives to people whose names one doesn't know."

"But why should the Admiral have introduced you to the British Ambassador as a person whose name he didn't know when this MacOgg who was too mean to pay fifteen zlotys for having his shirts washed had already introduced you to the Admiral?"

"Because MacOgg didn't know my name either and so instead of introducing me to the Admiral he introduced the Admiral to me."

"And was it as the Admiral Sir David Doddick or as the Admiral Arbuthnot or George that the Admiral repaired to the Ambasada Chinskiej Republiki Ludowej at Number Five Aleja Róż in the company of the Chinese Ambassador?"

"As the Admiral Arbuthnot or George, I expect. The Admiral hadn't met the Chinese Ambassador before."

"Then why did the British Ambassador use the Chinese Ambassador's nickname Hoo Flung Dung when he asked him to go across and talk to the Chinese Ambassador?"

"Hoo Flung Dung's like Arbuthnot or George. Englishmen one doesn't know very well or whose names one doesn't know are Arbuthnots or Georges. Chinamen one doesn't know very well are Hoo Flung Dungs."

"Truly the English language has many treasures hidden in its vasty deeps. Anyway, Professor Hilliard or Mr. Arbuthnot or Whale, let me tell you this for the solace of your prevaricating heart. So far what you said to *Polska Prawda* has not been reported in the British press and although I do not for one minute believe your story about this MacOgg and his shirts it now looks highly probably that I shall be able to employ you in the secret service of our People's Democratic Republic."

Clearly it must have been only the Ambassador's conversation with the Admiral and not the Ambassador's with Hilliard which had been reported to Karminski. Karminski wouldn't be talking this way if he'd known that the Ambassador had read *Polska Prawda*. Surprised that Karminski hadn't thought of such a possibility, Hilliard did his best to keep a poker face: the best way of making Karminski want to do business with Hilliard was for Hilliard not to appear too eager to do business with Karminski.

"My price however has gone up. I now require to put in the picture not only about Sardine, but also about the Admiral and the Chinese Ambassador."

"How can I tell you what I don't know myself?"

"Come off it, Professor Hilliard. Why should the Admiral have introduced you to the British Ambassador as Mr. Arbuthnot if he himself were not another British agent?"

Things had taken a turn for the worse again and Hilliard could see no way out of this new predicament which coincidence had let him in for. Karminski might be persuaded that Sardine had gone to ground and that Hilliard hadn't been able to contact him. He might even be made to believe that for security reasons Hilliard had been kept in ignorance of the Admiral's business with the Chinese Ambassador. One story or the other Karminski might swallow, but certainly not both.

"In any case you have still a few days to think things over, Professor Hilliard. The fact that the British daily papers have not mentioned your interview with *Polska Prawda* does not mean that the Sunday ones will not, and it will be Tuesday at earliest before we can get down to brass tacks."

When Karminski had gone Hilliard looked at his watch. It was ten minutes past ten. Miss Zamoyska's telephoning had worked at last and he was able to shave without the bell ringing in his bedroom; but even if her telepathy had given him a bath plug he wouldn't have taken a bath: he couldn't risk arriving late at the cemetery gates. Sardine was the only person who could help him now.

10

Even less than the night before, Hilliard couldn't afford to take any chances by ordering a taxi from the doorman. Mastering his haste, he walked along the Marszałkowska until he was certain that no one was following him and then ran back to the taxi rank. *"Tak, Cmentarz Powązkowski,"* the driver said in answer to his instructions in English. Nobody seemed to be watching the cab as it drove off and nobody was getting into another cab behind. All Hilliard could see when he looked out of the rear window was pavements crowded with the anonymous spill of history and four, fifteen, nineteen and twenty-three red trams sailing up and down the Marszałkowska like yachts ticketed for a race.

His heart gave a jump when on another broad street with trams on it a policeman in a brown leather jacket and a white cap held up his hand and stopped them. It was however only a traffic control check, but the policeman took so long examining the driver's papers and testing the taxi's lamps and windscreen wipers that it was ten minutes to eleven by the time he had finished. Did a secret agent wait for another secret agent when the other secret agent was late? Hilliard wondered. Wouldn't it be against the rules for him to risk drawing attention to himself by loitering?

There were only eight and twenty-two trams in the next street they turned into. Soon the houses began to thin out into what was almost countryside. At two minutes to eleven the driver turned sharp left and a few seconds later drew up in front of iron gates. A man was standing outside them with just enough sandy hair showing above an unfolded newspaper for Hilliard to be able to recognize Sardine. Knowing that an empty taxi waiting outside the cemetery would be as good as a footprint to Karminski, Hilliard paid the driver off, trusting that one of the eight or twenty-two trams would get him at least part of the way back to the hotel.

"Please," he said as he walked up to the still unlowered *Trybuna Ludu,* "there's something I've simply got to make you understand."

"Don't be a fool. In this country even cemetery walls have ears." Sardine led Hilliard quickly through the gates and did not speak again until he stopped in front of a plot of rain-rotted wooden crosses. "Our 1920 war dead. Curious, isn't it? how much easier it is to love the fallen than the survivors. You're a Catholic of course, I take it?"

"Only in so far as the Church of England manages to think me one."

"That's funny. Caviare generally sends R.C.'s out here, but perhaps the supply has dried up."

"That's just what I wanted to talk to you about. Caviare didn't—"

"Careful." When Hilliard looked over his shoulder he understood the reason for Sardine's warning. Lined up behind them was a squad of expressionless men in blue uniforms which looked so like policemen's that Hilliard's first thought was that they must have been sent by Karminski to arrest himself and Sardine. But when the men had stood and stared for a little at the graves with respectful boredom they moved on up the hill.

"A railwaymen's pilgrimage," Sardine explained. "But one never knows: Bekas is up to all the dodges, so perhaps we'd better keep on walking slowly for a little before you start giving me the gen." The railwaymen had shrunk into a blot of ink on the horizon by the time Sardine stopped at a plot of newer wooden crosses garlanded with ribbons and flowers like country girls' hats at a fair.

"The *Zośka* battalion," Sardine said. "Boys of sixteen to

twenty-five. Machine-gunned by the Germans in batches some of them and not always dead when they were buried. Anyway whatever they were stifled for, it wasn't for the new semantics of the West. Sanctity has never been sanctimoniousness in Poland nor sentiment sentimentality."

"We don't all of us think that way." Considering it bad taste to speak of his own problems while Sardine was lamenting his country's heroes, Hilliard gazed out over the soldiers sleeping their young Polish deaths in the same tight files as Northumberlands and Argylls at Etaples, numbered off into eternity as though they had fallen in on parade.

"Easy again with the English for a moment; there's a chap coming this way who looks as though he might just possibly be a stool pigeon." Padding along towards them was a railwayman all on his own, but he stood staring at the decorated crosses with tears in his eyes, and he didn't follow Sardine and Hilliard when they moved on to yet another set of graves.

"The Eight Girl Martyrs," Sardine said. "That verse you see on the tombstone is the song they sang when they were led out to be shot. Will the victims of Polaris and Minuteman go to their deaths with a song on their lips—will they even if they have the time?"

How was it that Sardine spoke English like an Englishman? Hilliard wondered. Had he had an English mother?

"And now, Whale, to save us both going on making targets of ourselves like this I'll tell you what you've come to tell me. Caviare's right: I've been dragging my feet; but what he doesn't know is that I've been dragging them purposely. Tell him from me I'm no longer playing. If Caviare wants to know the location of Russian Intercontinental Ballistic Missile launching sites all he's got to do is to send Kipper sailing over them in a satellite with a Brownie—I'm not letting the Lublin Children of Mary risk their necks for Ascot and coffee bars. And this I think is where I fade out—two's company, three hundred and thirty-three's none." As Sardine walked rapidly away in one direction a horde of pink ticketed matchfolder collectors came swooping along the path from the other.

The Admiral detached himself from the pilgrims and strode up to Hilliard.

"Tell me, Arbuthnot, I hope you remembered to ask for MacOggski's shirts when you left the party last night because I didn't."

"I forgot too, I'm afraid."

"Then the only thing for me to do is ring up Nodder and hope he manages to get the shirts back to me before Mac-Oggski starts asking me about them. So far he hasn't said a word but probably only because he hasn't yet recovered from Bacchus and Venus, so for heaven's sake keep him off the subject if you can." The Admiral left hastily as MacOgg sauntered up.

"Man, this is a gey dreich place for pleesure. Minds me of a riddle I once heard. When ye gang into a cemetery at night what is it ye can hear the deid folk saying? Ye give up? Well, Ah'll tell ye. When ye gang into a cemetery at night ye can hear the deid folk saying: 'Nae-thing! Nae-thing! Nae-thing!' Of course the deid folk arena saying naething at all because they canna open their mooths and that's how they're saying nae-thing. Good one, isn't it, Mac?"

Hilliard was much too worried by Sardine's flight to pretend to be amused. Unless he managed to overtake Sardine before he reached the gates of the cemetery he was lost. The main body of the matchfolder collectors was now standing in front of the Eight Girl Martyrs' grave, at degrees of attention diminishing from the Admiral's. Without a word of explanation to MacOgg, Hilliard left him and ran.

But whether because Sardine had run faster or had jumped a wall he wasn't anywhere to be seen when Hilliard came rushing out through the gates. On the chance that Sardine might be hiding until the matchfolder collectors had moved on to another part of the cemetery, Hilliard decided to wait. Half an hour later Sardine still hadn't put in an appearance, and Hilliard was on the point of giving up and boarding a tram when a motor scooter came freewheeling down the center path. On the scooter was Hippolyte who coasted up to Hilliard and said:

"So Monsieur too has been visiting Poland's glorious dead?" The spaced out teeth were like exclamation marks to emphasize the sincerity of the hyperbole—visiting the glorious dead apparently was not inconsistent with trying to prod customers into bed with the glorious living.

Hilliard gladly accepted Hippolyte's offer of a lift back to the Leningrad on the carrier of his scooter; but Hippolyte rode so speedily that Hilliard was glad of the rest when the traffic policeman who had stopped the taxi on the way out held them up to go through his rigmarole.

"I reminded him that he had checked me half an hour ago, but it was no use," Hippolyte grumbled as they rode on again, more slowly until they were out of sight of the traffic policeman. "The same thing happened to me last Sunday when I was out with my wife. My wife, Monsieur, is a very nice wife, and I have always been faithful to her."

Another of those Polish islands of fidelity, Hilliard thought, but did not make any comment.

"Perhaps that is why Monsieur did not accept the invitation of Mademoiselle Halina the other night. Perhaps Monsieur too has always been faithful to his wife."

"Only because temptation and opportunity have never coincided so commendation would be inappropriate."

"*Ah, ces Anglais!* Anyway Monsieur will be glad to hear that I have good news for him. I have already telephoned to Mademoiselle Halina and she confirms that it is at eleven o'clock that she will be waiting for him at the Café Manekin tonight. She also asks me to assure Monsieur that this time she will see to it that she is alone."

Although grateful for this information, Hilliard was too disturbed by his failure to obtain help from Sardine to accord it much importance. If Karminski wasn't going to allow Hilliard to return to England until he had betrayed a man whose identity he didn't know and revealed a non-existent plot it didn't look as though the £298 : 9 : 0 to pay Catacomb and Priddle's commission were going to be of more practical use than the £176 : 11 : 0 not to tell the Inland Revenue about.

But the smile Miss Zamoyska gave him when he entered the front hall of the Leningrad was so radiant that it all but banished the fears which had made him forget his lunch appointment with her.

11

"You see now how popular your book is in Poland," Miss Zamoyska said as she drew Hilliard's attention to the boot-black who looked like Piłsudski with his nose stuck in *Symfonia Dysonansów*. "Of course I don't know if all your readers appreciate just how clever you've been."

What a change from Charlotte! Charlotte had never taken the slightest interest in what he wrote, far less shown that she'd thought him clever.

"And you're so right about the Dysteleological Surd," Miss Zamoyska went on as she tugged off her coat and handed it in a ball to the cloakroom attendant. "Why should it always be Poland that hangs like Christ on the Cross between two thieves? Why should it never be Switzerland?" The little india-rubber face was corrugated with concern.

"There you have me cornered." But even the comic aspect of Miss Zamoyska's lilac sweater and scarlet woolen stockings couldn't dispel the effect of the morning's tribulations. Only vodka could do that, and Hilliard was in such a hurry to feel its impact that he almost pushed the girl into a small deserted bar opening off the main hall.

"I can drink today all right as I'm not driving," Miss Zamoyska said as she perched on a stool and showed her clamant knees. "Tell me: did you get that thought I sent out to you the night before last about why I wasn't at your lecture?"

"Of course." Wanting to give her pleasure, Hilliard made the best guess he could. "As soon as I saw you weren't at the press table I realized in a blinding flash that you'd been sent to interview some other visiting fireman."

"What sort of other visiting fireman?"

"A French Communist politician."

"Wrong. A British matchfolder collector: Admiral Sir David Doddick. And in any case your realizing in a blinding flash ought to have taken place before you left the hotel for your lecture which was when I sent you out the thought. You can see for yourself: it didn't work at all." The misery on her mouth was so great that Hilliard didn't mind how much he had to go on lying to console it.

"Anyway I can tell you a thought sending out of yours that did work. You remember that missing bath plug of mine you sent a thought down to the concierge about? Well, there was a new plug on the chain when I went to bed that night and the telephone bell you rang down about wasn't mended till the next afternoon."

"How do you know the maid didn't notice that the plug was missing when she made down your bed, and call the house plumber?"

"For the simple reason that she didn't make down my bed— I had to take off the cover and draw the curtains myself. And the bathroom hadn't been tidied."

"Then it *did* work! Do you know, I think it's the first *concrete* proof I've ever had. Thank you! Thank you! Thank you!" The smile she gave him was so ecstatic and the hand she pressed briefly into his so soft that they did almost as much as the vodka to numb Hilliard's dread of Karminski.

"It is better to laugh than to weep, is it not, *M'sieu et Dame*?" Hippolyte said as he pulled out their chairs for them in the restaurant. While Miss Zamoyska was doing the ordering for them both Halina came mincing down on her way to the other bar and as she passed their table pouted at Hilliard the silent syllables: "MANE-KIN RY-NEK STAR-E-GO MI-ASTA."

"That's the girl that was making those eyes at you the other night, isn't it?" Miss Zamoyska said as she handed the menu back to Hippolyte. "Don't think I didn't notice. I expect it's your soldierly appearance that attracts her. Tell me: did you do very heroic things for your country during the war?"

"Not really." Except for having stood ready to repel German tanks with a revolver he hadn't known how to fire, the most heroic thing Hilliard had done during the war had been to threaten to report O.C. "D" Coy, 3d Shropshire Fusiliers, to his Battalion Commander unless he forwarded his petty cash vouchers by return of post. Even then it had been R.F.C. Bircumshaw, Lieutenant and Paymaster, who had signed the letter.

"Only because you weren't lucky enough to have the opportunity, I'm sure. I didn't have the opportunity either of course: when the war was over I was only five. But I'm ready to dare anything now in defence of the Two Cultures."

"Literature and science, you mean?" So it had been Snowing over here too, had it?

"Marxism and theology, I mean. I know they're generally considered to be incompatible, but all that's wrong with Marxism is its theology and all that's wrong with the Church is its economics. Once Khrushchev and the Pope get that into their nuts there'll be no more Iron Curtain and no more Cold War."

"Berdyaev's not quite so optimistic," Hilliard said gently. "Berdyaev thinks that Christians and the world will go on betraying each other till the end of time."

"Berdyaev isn't the new St. Thomas of Aquin like Teilhard de Chardin is. Teilhard de Chardin says that man is progressing all the time towards universal spirituality. The only thing he didn't seem to know was that the next jumping off ground was going to be Poland."

"*Pamiętasz Capri i nasze spotkanie.*" Bouncing round the main bar neither the Admiral nor Halina seemed to be bothering about universal spirituality or the new St. Thomas of Aquin.

"Of course the proper people to tell you about this are the monks at Kłock. I could take you over to see them tomorrow if you like: it's Saturday and I'm sure the newspaper would let me have the morning off and lend me a car. We'd have to start from here about ten though, but I expect you'd find it well worth while. For one thing the monks will be able to give you all the details about the deal between Gomulka and Cardinal Wyszyński."

However that wasn't why Hilliard accepted; he accepted because he wanted to spend a day alone in a car with Miss Zamoyska. *"Pamiętasz Capri i nasze spotkanie?"* Although all six of Hilliard's bracer clips had given before they had done one twirl round the bar, vodka was now making the top of his trousers fit as tightly as a belt. "Do you remomber Cap Rye and the lost time we mat?" Karminski could think Hilliard was Kipper as well as Whale if he liked—Hilliard was ready to be the soldierly man Miss Zamoyska had said he looked. *"Pamiętasz Capri i nasze spotkanie?"* Before they had returned to their table he was calling her Wanda.

12

But as soon as Wanda left him, Hilliard's courage evaporated and he began to tremble again. How could he be sure that Karminski hadn't intruded a spy among the railwaymen or matchfolder collector pilgrims to the cemetery and that he wasn't already informed about Hilliard's meeting with Sardine? Soldierly appearance notwithstanding, Hilliard knew that he was only an intellectual without enough iodine in his blood. Karminski had only to show him the tools of his trade and Hilliard would break down completely and sell as much of the pass as it was in his power to sell.

Afraid of being followed if he went for a walk, he stayed in his room till dinner time. On his way down to the restaurant, he picked up and put in his pocket a matchfolder collector's pink ticket which he found lying in the corridor, deciding to wear it in his lapel when he went to the Manekin. If by any chance his and Halina's exchange of banknotes were observed, it was preferable that he should be taken for an anonymous delegate to the convention than identified with the badgeless author of a Polish best seller.

Hilliard arrived at the Manekin at eleven o'clock sharp. Halina was sitting alone at one of the small tables. When he had made sure that neither the Admiral nor MacOgg was lurking in the tobacco fog he went up to her and said the only three words he knew in Polish:

"Tualeta—Męski Damski." Provided both compartments were free, the lavatory seemed the safest place to carry out their deal.

"Wiśniowka," Halina said, and there was nothing Hilliard could do but sit down beside her.

But even when she had had her cherry brandy Halina seemed to be in no hurry to come to the point, and to remind her of the purpose of their meeting Hilliard repeated his basic Polish:

"Tualeta—Męski Damski."

At this instant all the lights in the café went out. A hubbub greeted the darkness and a pile of banknotes was pushed across the table into Hilliard's hands. It wasn't the way Hilliard had wanted the transaction to take place, but if Halina was willing to trust him he would have to trust Halina. Unloading his pockets and wallet as quickly as he could he dumped his zlotys under the table into Halina's lap. He had just finished doing this when the lights went on again and his arms were seized roughly from behind. A policeman snatched the pound and dollar notes still lying on top of the table and another two frog-marched Hilliard up the stairs and pushed him into a car that was waiting outside.

13

A few minutes later the car drew up at a door with MIEJSKA KOMENDA MILICJI OBYWATELSKIEJ above it in lighted letters. After waiting for a little in a dilapidated room with a policeman as guard Hilliard was hustled into an office in which Karminski was seated at a desk with two piles of banknotes in front of him. The policeman went out and left them alone together.

"A thousand dollars, one hundred and twenty odd pounds, that is a lot of money for a professor of philosophy to be rolling in, Professor Hilliard. Perhaps you would be kind enough to show me the foreign currency declaration which you had stamped at Okecie airport on your arrival."

While Karminski was examining the document Hilliard did a rapid sum in his head: a thousand dollars at seventy zlotys to the dollar came to seventy thousand zlotys, one hundred and twenty pounds odd at two hundred zlotys to the pound anything above twenty thousand zlotys—whatever shortage there might be was too insignificant for the mistake to have been other than a genuine slip up. His explanation therefore must be one which didn't involve Halina whose fault it certainly wasn't that Karminski had been clever enough to have Hilliard followed to the Manekin without his having noticed. To say that the money represented her fee would be ridiculous: even old men with a foot in the grave didn't have to pay as dearly as that for their pleasures. The only way out seemed to be an elaboration of the lie he had told Witkowski. He could say that the dollars and sterling were a down payment on a fur coat for Charlotte which he had been asking

Halina, as an expert, to buy for him. Fur coats were notoriously expensive and could easily have eaten up his zloty royalties as well as the foreign currency. The nondeclaration he could attribute to his fear of drawing the attention of the British customs authorities to his illegal export of dollars and excessive sterling. Then he saw that this story wouldn't hold water either: and could easily be disproved: nothing had obliged him to fill in his currency declaration before leaving London, and Halina, who would certainly be interrogated, would be caught unprepared to substantiate his lie.

"As I expected, not a sausage. The only amounts inscribed here are £100 in traveler's checks and £9 : 17 : 10 in coin. Why is that?"

"I must have forgotten, I suppose."

"I do not think that you forgot. I think that you remembered to forget." Karminski stared for a long time in silence at the lapel of Hilliard's overcoat. "Why did you not also disguise yourself as a matchfolder collector when you went to meet the Admiral at the Tomb of the Eight Girl Martyrs in the Powązki military cemetery this morning?"

"I didn't go to the Powązki military cemetery to meet the Admiral; I went to the Powązki military cemetery to see the war graves. My bumping into the Admiral at the Tomb of the Eight Girl Martyrs was quite accidental." Hilliard tried to derive what consolation he could from the thought that Karminski's charge might very well have been a much more serious one. Karminski had had his spy in the cemetery all right, but disguised as a matchfolder collector and not as a railwayman, otherwise it would have been Sardine that Hilliard would have been accused of having gone to meet.

"Why do you go on lying to me, Professor Hilliard? The reason you went to the Powązki military cemetery this morning was not to visit war graves but to tip the Admiral the wink about the questions I had just been asking you about his visit to Number Five Aleja Róż in the company of the Chinese Ambassador."

"Why should I have chosen a roundabout way like that? If I had wanted to tip the Admiral off about anything why couldn't I have rung him up or gone to see him in his room?"

"Because you had learned from bitter experience that I have many friends in your hotel who would instantly have reported either of these activities to me on the dot. But you knew that the matchfolder collectors were making a pilgrimage to the Powązki military cemetery this morning and so you had the brain wave of meeting him there beneath the weeping willows."

Was Karminski asking all those questions about the Admiral so as to be able to return to the foreign currency offence with greater impact when he had deluded Hilliard into imagining that he had forgotten all about it? Such, Hilliard knew, was the technique of the Soviets at International Conferences. But from the very beginning of Hilliard's association with him, Karminski had been voluble about his distrust of the Admiral. Had the Admiral's departure from the reception with the Chinese Ambassador been as innocent of subversive purpose as Hilliard had imagined? Could Caviare be trying to use Chinese deviation as he had obviously been trying to use Polish religious discontent? Had Karminski been as right about the Admiral as he had been wrong about Hilliard? Was the Admiral the agent called Kipper whom Sardine had wanted Caviare to send sailing over Soviet Inter-Continental Ballistic Missile launching sites with a Brownie?

"I have ascertained that when you and the Admiral arrived to attend the reception at the British Embassy one of you was in fact carrying a laundry bag. But it was not *you* who were carrying it as you gave me to understand. On the contrary it was the Admiral himself who was carrying it."

"I was carrying it to begin with. The Admiral only took over at the door of the Embassy to make it easier for me to fish in my pocket for money to pay the taxi with."

"Let us not split hairs. When you had been greeted like long lost brothers by the British Ambassador it was the Admiral who handed the laundry bag to the cloakroom attendant. So far so good. But I have also ascertained that neither the Admiral nor yourself asked the cloakroom attendant for the bag when you left. Why was that? I can only conclude that it was because the contents of the laundry bag were not shirts at all but top secret instructions to His Excellency from M.I.5."

"The things you manage to think up!" But Karminski's suggestion was scarcely more absurd than the truth: that the Admiral and he had gone to an official reception at the British Embassy carrying a laundry bag filled with a Scotsman's dirty shirts.

"That is my job, Professor Hilliard: to think up what the enemies of social progress have thought up against us." There was only one light in the room, the reading lamp on the desk with a green shade the shape of a skiing helmet, and the penumbra round Karminski's head made his thin lips look like a crack in plaster. "Why should the Admiral have taken the trouble to pay a visit to General de Gaulle in Paris before coming to Warsaw to attend the Matchfolder Collectors' Convention? The answer that I find is that it must have been in order to obtain additional secret know-how in order to stand a better chance of persuading the Chinese Ambassador that it was the West and not the East which was going to win the next shooting match."

"You've got it all taped, I see."

"Perhaps even more than you think. After you had spoken with the Admiral this morning in the Powązki military cemetery you lunched with the lady reporter from *Polska Prawda* in the restaurant of the Leningrad. As she had already interviewed you for her newspaper on the night of your arrival in Warsaw why did you require to see her a second time?"

"Because I happen to like her company, that's all. She's young and she's pretty and she's intelligent—a pleasant change from the whiskery old bags that are generally my lot at home."

"In other words you are now asking me to believe that you are a gay Lothario. Not only are you a bad liar, Professor

Hilliard, but you are also very clumsy. Famous philosophers who are interviewed by journalists give information to the journalists for the journalists to write down; they do not pocket information which the journalists have written down for the famous philosophers."

So he had been right after all: Karminski *had* been having them watched that first night in the restaurant. The only mistake Hilliard had made was to have imagined that it had been MacOgg who was the spy.

"The information your sleuth saw Miss Zamoyska write down for me was a list of the months in Polish. And as it was her way of thanking me for the interview I didn't like to hurt her feelings by telling her about the one you'd already written out for me on the plane."

It wasn't until he'd taken the list out of his wallet and handed it to Karminski that Hilliard remembered the calculations he'd made on the back. If Karminski were to notice them not only would he know that Hilliard's black market deal with Halina had been premeditated but he might also conclude that Wanda had been a party to it. All Hilliard could do was to close his eyes and will that Karminski would give him back the piece of paper without turning it over to see if there was anything written on the other side. His telepathy however was as unsuccessful as Wanda's about the missing bath plug.

"These three sums here, Professor Hilliard—what do they represent?"

"I was trying to work out how much commission I owed my literary agents and how much I'd have left over for myself afterwards. Nineteen percent is what I've got to pay the blighters, and in sterling too, worse luck."

"In that case why is there no calculation of that percentage here? And why is it the bigger sum instead of the lesser which is subtracted from the ninety-five thousand zlotys? And why is the multiplier in the first sum and the divisor in the third two hundred instead of sixty-seven which is the rate which the Narodowy Bank Polski would allow you if it granted you a permit to take your zloty royalties back to England in sterling? And why does the ninety-five thousand zlotys in the second sum from which you have subtracted the product of the first sum equal as near as makes no difference the black market value of these pounds and dollars which I have here in front of me on this desk? To me the answer is as clear as the address written above the calculations. The multiplicand of £298 : 9 : 0 in the first sum represents an installment of sterling salary and bonus due by Her Gracious Majesty Good Queen Bess the Second to her loyal secret agent Sardine. The quotient of £176 : 11 : 0 in the third sum represents the black market sterling value of the zlotys still left over from those which you would have received from the Since October girl for your pounds and dollars had our loyal Polish coppers not turned up in time to prevent the deal taking place. To this second lot of zlotys no doubt you were going to have to add a proportion of your zloty royalties in order to make up the black market value of yet another installment of sterling salary and bonus earned by Sardine. And the reason you did not inscribe these pounds and dollars on your currency declaration was because you did not wish to draw the attention of the Polish customs authorities to imports of money which were too big to be spent in ten days but none of which would be in your possession when you left the country again."

Hilliard began to regret that Halina had been so honest. If she had shortchanged him by a hundred pounds or so, he would have had no compunction in letting her bear her share of the guilt. Karminski could then have been asked to confirm with Witkowski that the royalties he had paid Hilliard yesterday had amounted to ninety-five thousand zlotys. Changing zlotys into black market dollars and pounds in order to pay Catacomb and Priddle their commission might be a hostile act against the foreign currency reserves of the Narodowy Bank Polski, but the offence would have been a peccadillo compared with the crime of which he was now being accused.

"And what could be more fitting than that these calculations should have been worked out on the back of the list of the Polish months which Sardine herself has written out for you her own fair hand?"

Hilliard was so appalled by the significance of this new accusation that it was a second or two before he could speak.

"So Miss Zamoyska's Sardine now, is she? Good God, Mr. Karminski, if you'll believe nonsense like that you'll believe anything."

"It is not nonsense, as I think that you are the first to know. A reporter working on the staff of a Polish newspaper—it is just what the doctor ordered for a cover story for a British secret agent operating in Poland. And how easy it makes it for you to give an interview about the Western Slide to Death and try to double-cross me by pretending to be a fellow traveler in search of a job."

"False premises, undistributed middles—has anyone ever taught you the elementary principles of logic? Miss Zamoyska's no more Sardine than Gomulka is."

"If you yourself are not Whale how can you know who is not Sardine?"

"By using my common sense, that's all. Miss Zamoyska's little more than a schoolgirl. She's far too young to be involved in cloak and dagger business."

"It is amazing what schoolgirls can be involved in these days—far too much anyway for me to risk offering you employment. That you must now regard as out. Nevertheless I am still willing to do a deal with you. Admit that it is Miss Zamoyska who is Sardine and I shall trouble you no more. I shall also ask you no more questions about the Admiral and I shall allow you to return to England with a clean copy book. Nobody will ever learn from me that you have betrayed a member of your network. All that you will require to do when you arrive home will be to tell your Big White Chief that you were unable to contact Sardine because she had been arrested, which by that time will be true. And to make sure that your Big White Chief believes you I shall give you back these dollars and pounds which you brought over to pay her salary. Come clean with me, Professor Hilliard. It is Miss Zamoyska who is Sardine, is it not?"

Hilliard was tempted. By speaking out now he could save both Wanda and himself. Wanda meant more to him than a sandy haired little man whom he had only met twice and vaguely liked. Wouldn't he be co-operating less with the Dysteleological Surd by denouncing Sardine who was guilty than by allowing Wanda who was innocent to go on being suspected? The answer, he couldn't escape it, was that he would be co-operating more with the Dysteleological Surd by denouncing Sardine because he would be saving his own skin as well as Wanda's. It was almost with relief therefore that he realized that he couldn't denounce Sardine even if he wanted to because he knew neither Sardine's real name nor address, and Karminski would never believe that Hilliard hadn't been told at least one or the other.

"And quite apart from assuring your personal safety, Professor Hilliard, you might as well save us both time and trouble by telling me now what as sure as God made little apples I shall find out for myself before very much more water has passed under the bridge."

"The bridge will no longer be standing by the time you find out that Miss Zamoyska is Sardine."

"All right, Professor Hilliard. As you refuse to co-operate with me your blood must now be on your own head." Karminski pressed a bell on the desk and two of the policemen who had arrested Hilliard came into the room. "These gentlemen will now conduct you back to your hotel. It will of course be useless for you to attempt to leave Poland without my consent. In the meantime I am hanging on to these pounds and dollars and the calculations relating thereto. They will be my official reason for throwing you into one of our dungeons in the Mugatal should your obstinacy force me to take such a course. Goodnight, Professor Hilliard. Sleep tight. Mind the fleas don't bite."

14

Next morning Hilliard flopped out of bed determined to implement the unpleasant decision he had come to in the bar the night before: for Wanda's sake alone the trip to Kłock would have to be canceled. Although Karminski's alternation of cajoling and threats had shown that Karminski wasn't as certain as he had pretended to be that Wanda was Sardine, his suspicion might very well become conviction if Wanda were to be seen any more in the company of a man he was positive was Whale. Hilliard wouldn't however tell Wanda his real reason for scrapping their outing: he had done her enough harm as it was without frightening her into the bargain. He would say that Witkowski had made a last minute appointment for him which he couldn't get out of. The rest, as Karminski would probably say, was on the knees of the gods.

Anxious that the image which Wanda retained of him should be flattering, Hilliard applied his electric razor to his ears as well as to his chin and cheeks; and although Wanda's thought-sending-out hadn't yet given him a bath plug, by stuffing the hole with his face cloth he managed to keep the water in the bath long enough to be able to wash his whole body.

Punctually at ten o'clock, the swing door ejected Wanda into the front hall. As soon as she caught sight of Hilliard, her face lit up and she broke into a run. Watching her unbuttoned coat flare out like a skirt as she galloped up to him, Hilliard realized how fond he had become of her. Giving up going to Kłock with her was going to be more difficult than he had imagined, but for Wanda's sake at least, the sacrifice would have to be made.

"Our trip's off I'm afraid." Hilliard looked her as straight in the eyes as he dared. "Last night that blighter of a publisher of mine rang up to say that he'd arranged some sort of official reception for me this morning at the Warsaw Pen Club and I can't very well let him down. I'd have saved you the bother of coming all this way for nothing if I'd known your telephone number and there were so many other Zamoyskas in the book I didn't know which was which."

"This morning the Warsaw Pen Club is being addressed by the French novelist Petitpiquier. The reason I know is because I was going to have been sent to cover his lecture if I hadn't got permission to take you to Kłock. But even if it bores you to go out with me perhaps you'll allow me to have a cup of coffee with you in the *Kawiarnia* instead." There was no reproach on her mournful face.

"Of course, of course."

She was off along the corridor before Hilliard could attempt to explain his clumsy lie, shedding her coat to reveal another liquorice allsort getup: grey flannel skirt, white woolen stockings and a pale blue jumper under a pink cardigan. Her knitted green hat was like a pewter fruit bowl and when Hilliard sat down opposite her at the small table she had chosen, her eyelashes were sparkling with tears.

"I know I'm being silly, but I can't help it." She whipped out a red handkerchief the size of a small flag and blew her nose so loudly that all the matchfolder collectors near them turned round and stared. "You've no idea how much I was looking forward to our day in the country together. It was to have been a sort of Absolute for me, but of course I can understand a clever man like you not wanting to waste his time with an empty-headed girl like me."

"You've got hold of the wrong end of the stick." Hilliard's whole heart went out to her miserable little face and to the cedilla of hair crawling out from the edge of her hat like a snail. "It's just that I don't think that it'd have been very wise."

"You mean you're afraid that you might have been tempted to make love to me." The creases beginning to appear at the corners of her mouth showed Hilliard that he'd found an excuse for cancelling their trip which wouldn't hurt her feelings.

"That's it." And when he had ordered coffee for them both in German he elaborated. "I'm a devil for the women, there's no other word for it. And going out with a pretty girl like you might put ideas into my head."

"I shouldn't worry too much about that if I were you. After all some of the most holy saints weren't able to keep carnal images out of their minds even in *spiritual* ecstasies—asking God to pierce the marrow of their soul with the delicious and health-giving dart of His love and that sort of thing."

"That's just the point. I'm not a saint and the carnal images might be too much for me."

"At Kłock there'd be too many monks about for you to yield to them and except for when I had to slow up in towns and villages I'd be driving at more than a hundred miles an hour and that's rather off-putting for carnal images. I think it's very noble of you to reveal your lowest depths like this, but there's no need for you to give way to despair. Meister Eckhart says that it's only by watching the serpent of our own filth wind its way out of us that we can hope to attain perfection."

"I'm afraid the whole serpent's not out yet." There was nothing else for it, Hilliard saw: he would have to tell Wanda at least a portion of the truth.

"Even if you've taken part in orgies that's still no reason for you to give way to despair. Despair's a much worse sin than orgies. St. Augustine took part in orgies and he ended up a bishop."

"It's not something I've done; it's something I'm suspected of having done or rather of doing." After making sure that none of the matchfolder collectors in their neighborhood looked as though he or she were listening, Hilliard told Wanda about the mistakes with the suitcase and the overcoat which had led Karminski to imagine that Hilliard was a British agent called Whale.

"But how exciting! I've always wanted to meet a spy." Wanda's voice rang out across the terraces of bacon and eggs and corn on the cob even more loudly than her nose-blow. "For of course you *are* Whale, aren't you? Naturally you can still go on saying you're not even if you are: the Church allows one to lie in defence of one's country."

"For God's sake, child! Do you want to get us both arrested?" But the matchfolder collectors, apparently knowing no French, had already turned back to their munching.

"ALL RIGHT THEN I'LL WHISPER." She brought her chubby face half way across the table and aspirated at him hoarsely: "SURELY THE BEST THING FOR YOU TO DO IS TO SHOUT OUT AT THE TOP OF YOUR VOICE THAT YOU ARE WHALE AND THEN EVERYBODY WILL THINK THAT YOU AREN'T."

"Unfortunately that particular dodge seems to have been rather overworked lately. And however much it disappoints you I'm not Whale—really and truly I'm not. But the fact that Karminski thinks I am makes it dangerous for you to be seen in my company and that's the real reason why I want to call off our trip to Kłock."

"I'm not afraid if you aren't." Her whole face was rippling with toughness: St. Catherine of Siena had been bulldozed away by Tugboat Annie.

"Can't you understand? If I go to Kłock with you it won't be only me Karminski takes for a spy; it'll be you as well."

"I don't mind. I'm not a spy. And Karminski's thinking I am can't make me one."

"That's just where you're wrong. With Karminski thinking is knowing. Karminski thinks that I'm Whale. Therefore Karminski *knows* that I'm Whale. In fact he knows so much that I'm Whale that he's told me that it'll be useless for me to leave Poland without his permission. He must have given orders to the people at the airport. Probably to all the frontier posts as well."

"All the more reason then for us going to Kłock. The monks are specialists in getting people out of that kind of jam. They saved masses of Jews from Auschwitz and Treblinka during the war. They'll be able to think up something for you too, I'm sure."

Hilliard now saw that he would have to frighten her properly.

"In that case we'd better ask them to help you as well. I didn't want to have to tell you, but now you've forced me to. Karminski's got his suspicions about you already and if I go to Kłock with you they'll probably turn into one of those devastating certainties of his I've just been speaking about. And that won't be funny at all."

"You mean he thinks I'm Whale-ess?" Not only was there no fright on her face but whatever concern there had been there before had been swamped by laughter. "If he's as stupid as that what does it matter what he thinks?"

"A great deal. Haven't I yet got it into your head that with Karminski thinking is *knowing?* Sardine's the name of the agent you're supposed to be and what makes it really serious is that Sardine, whoever he or she may be, is suspected of aiding and abetting Whale to stir up religious discontent in Poland. Therefore a monastery's the last place for us to be seen in each other's company."

"The man must be mad. It's religious *content* the monks are trying to stir up. Of course for the moment the Vatican's against them but in the end they'll be rehabilitated like St. Joan of Arc and Galileo when the Church thinks it safe to say it knew all along they were right."

"That won't be much help to you if Karminski runs you in for visiting them in my company."

"I'm not afraid to die for my religion if you are." Tugboat Annie had been replaced by a Regimental Sergeant-Major, Brigade of Guards, not Rush-rush.

"Dying for your religion's one thing; having your toenails torn out for no reason at all is another. You'd be a traitor to your own cause if you allowed that to happen. You'd be depriving Poland of a missionary. It's your duty as a patriot to divert suspicion from yourself."

"All right. I'll tell you what. I'll send out a thought to Karminski to think that I'm not Sardine and that you're not Whale." At first Hilliard imagined that she must be joking, but when she propped her chin on her fists and screwed up her face as though repressing a sneeze he wasn't so sure. "There! I've sent it out. We ought both of us to be as safe as houses now."

"I thought that for telepathy to work properly the sender out of the message had to know the recipient."

"My message about your missing bath plug reached the concierge here all right, didn't it?" If she *wasn't* joking, it was because of his lie. *Beware of Pity,* Hilliard remembered, had been the title of a novel by Stefan Zweig.

"That's scarcely a parallel: you'd already spoken to the concierge on the telephone about the bell ringing in my bedroom while I was shaving."

"That's just where you're wrong. I sent down the thought about the bath plug before I spoke on the telephone about the bell ringing. And in any case speaking to a person on the telephone can't be called knowing him. Naturally the fact that my telepathy has worked with one person doesn't necessarily mean that it will work with another, but I'm willing to take the risk if you are."

Hilliard saw that if he went on trying to dissuade her much longer she would end up by thinking that he had got cold feet and was concealing fear for his own person under a pretence of concern for hers. Those with soldierly appearances were expected to behave like soldiers. And mightn't going openly with Wanda to Kłock have consequences quite other than those he had just been prophesying? A man who could mistake a Scotsman's dirty shirts for top secret instructions from M.I.5 might just as easily interpret defiance as innocence. The munching matchfolder collectors looked so reassuringly stupid that Hilliard was almost able to imagine himself back in the common room having his elevenses; and the flecks of sunshine dancing in Wanda's eyes told him that he would be a fool if he passed up the chance of spending a day alone in the country with such a pretty girl.

"All right," he said. "We'll risk it."

15

The car which *Polska Prawda* had lent Wanda was a Polish Syrena. Hilliard sat in front with Wanda. On the outskirts of the town he saw a heron alighting on the Vistula and was so elated by the beauty of its silver swoop that he was almost able to forget the trouble he was in with Karminski.

As soon as they were clear of the town Wanda drove quickly. The narrow road was as black and glossy as a sailor's oilskins and the only traffic on it, carts drawn by horses with the gentle faces of saints. At a signpost marked KATOWICE 286 a traffic policeman stopped them, but even when he had finished his lengthy checks and tests there was still no other car in view on the gaunt stretch of steppe behind them.

Confident at last that they weren't being followed, Hilliard was able to notice that the face of a fat priest hurrying through the crowded street of a country town resembled the huge cheese he was carrying. Once they passed a cemetery with lighted candles planted round new graves like daffodils, often cows tethered to trees at the side of the road and twice a peasant leading a pig by a chain attached to one of its hind legs. Hilliard was sorrier for the cows and the pigs than for the new dead in their graves because he knew that the sufferings of animals formed the greater part of the Dysteleological Surd and that no theologian had ever succeeded in explaining them.

At one o'clock they arrived in a town called Drujsk full of office blocks as depressingly functional as girls in jeans. Wanda drove straight to a dank hotel. She and Hilliard were the only guests in the sour dining room and as soon as he had had a couple of vodkas, Hilliard began to wish that he were twenty years younger and not tied to Charlotte's semi-literacy and celanese bloomers.

"WHATEVER YOU DO DON'T LOOK ROUND." Wanda was leaning across the table and mouthing at him in the same throaty whisper as she had used in the Leningrad. "THERE'S A MAN JUST COME IN WHO LOOKS LIKE A POLICEMAN AND HE'S STANDING STARING AT US. HOLD MY HAND AS TIGHTLY AS YOU CAN AND THEN PERHAPS HE'LL THINK WE'RE ONLY LOVERS."

Hilliard's concupiscence subsided at once and even the warmth of Wanda's soft hand failed to rekindle it. If the worst had happened and the man who had come in was Karminski, Hilliard didn't see how pretending to be lovers was going to throw him off the scent.

"Darling, you mustn't ever again say that you're too old for me. It's brains I'm interested in, not callow youth." The words were trumpeted at him like curses from a rowing coach and the stage whisper which followed them was scarcely less audible. "NOW YOU SAY SOMETHING PASSIONATE TO ME—YOU KNOW, THE SORT OF THING YOU USED TO SAY TO YOUR WIFE WHEN YOU WERE ENGAGED."

What *had* he said to Charlotte in those dim days when her body had still been a guess for him? Muck about her eyes being like pansies probably—brass tacks had been out.

"AND DON'T FORGET TO CALL ME 'CHÉRIE'. THAT'S A FRENCH WORD EVEN THE STUPIDEST POLISH POLICEMAN UNDERSTANDS."

"Chérie, I love you so much I'd die for you!" Charlotte's answer to that sort of statement, he remembered, had been that she didn't like young men who were "sloppy".

"And I love you so much I'd jump from the roof of the Palac Kultury i Nauki for you! FALSE ALARM, I THINK. ANYWAY HE'S SITTING DOWN NOW AND NOT STARING AT US ANY MORE. BUT PERHAPS WE'D BETTER GO ON HOLDING HANDS JUST IN CASE."

As Hilliard's fear of Karminski diminished, the feel of Wanda's warm flesh against his began to have its classic effect.

By the time they were having their coffee he was finding it hard to believe that the tenderness he saw shining in her eyes was simulated. Intellectual girls after all often fell in love with men much older than themselves and the ravages of gerontophilia were not unknown at redbrick. Hilliard didn't come down to earth again until Wanda jerked her hand free and said they would have to hurry if they weren't to be late for vespers at the monastery.

Turning to follow her out of the restaurant, he had his first glimpse of the intruder who, to Hilliard's surprise, stood up and bowed. Interpreting the gesture as a Polish courtesy, Hilliard bowed back. As he did so, a sunbeam lit up the steel teeth of the policeman whose overcoat he had put on by mistake in East Berlin. Hilliard's first impulse was to try to brazen it out by going up and shaking hands. Then, deciding that shame was the proper demeanor for a man caught making love to a girl thirty years his junior, he averted his eyes and walked quickly on after Wanda.

16

A grey Citroën was drawn up behind the blue Syrena in front
of the hotel. Karminski, Hilliard realized, must have had a
spy disguised as a matchfolder collector listening in to his and
Wanda's conversation in the *Kawiarnia*. The spy had reported
to Karminski that they were on their way to visit the monastery
at Kłock and Karminski had sent his policeman friend to follow
them. But Hilliard kept his knowledge and his thoughts to
himself until they were well out of Drujsk and the continued
absence of the Citroën from the road behind them enabled
him to speak with a semblance of calm:

"Your first suspicions about that man were right. He's the
fellow whose overcoat I put on by mistake in East Berlin."

"I knew all along there was something fishy about him but
I saw that it was no good expecting you to make love to me
properly when you were frightened and that's why I said
that about the false alarm. Anyway it looks as though our act
has done the trick all right because there's not the slightest
speck showing in my reflector."

So the warmth in those curling fingers and the glow in those
starry eyes had been only charade after all. Hilliard was almost as distressed by this as he would have been by the news
that the policeman was pounding along behind them in his
Citroën.

"Of course I expect it's only me we've cleared. Men spies not
making love to girl spies doesn't mean that they don't to girls
who aren't spies. Probably the only reason your friend's given
up the chase is because he thinks you're too busy to be doing
any Whalery this afternoon. Which is just as well because it

87

gives us plenty of time to ask the monks for help for you."

Fear melted Hilliard's intestines again. Wanda was right: even if their lovemaking had cleared her, for Karminski and his colleague back in the dining room at Drujsk Hilliard was still Whale and nothing except the discovery of the real Whale was likely to make them think otherwise.

There was still no sign of the Citroën when they reached Kłock. The monks were already chanting in choir. At first Hilliard thought that it was the candle flames which were making Wanda's cheeks shine as she knelt in front of the carved Madonna with the face of a Girton principal, but when he looked closer he saw that it was tears. Clearly the news he had given her in the car had upset her more than she had been willing for him to see. Now that she knew who it was who had been watching them in the dining room did she really believe that their love-making act had been of any use at all or that the monks were going to be able to help either of them? Watching the candlelight turn her tears from silver to gold, Hilliard was sure that it was because she didn't that she was praying with such fervor.

As a philosopher Hilliard believed in prayer only when in the company of other philosophers who derided it; so he was glad when Wanda rose from her knees and led him down the church to a door labeled ZAKRYSTIA.

In the middle of the sacristy an acolyte was swinging a thurible filled with ignited charcoal, and as his head swerved to follow its trajectory, Hilliard saw with amazement that the pop eyes were Hippolyte's. He had barely recovered from this shock when the face of one of three monks who were vesting became Sardine's. As soon as he caught sight of Hilliard, Sardine shook his head warningly and then turned and smiled at Wanda.

"That's the priest I'm hoping will be able to help us," Wanda said, "but as he's officiating we'll have to wait till vespers are over."

"Monsieur is perhaps surprised to see me here," Hippolyte

said as he ambled over to greet Hilliard. "But like the Reverend Fathers I am convinced that religion is the only cure for Poland's woes."

Although Hilliard scarcely imagined that touting for Since October girls had been authorized by Cardinal Wyszyński in his deal with Gomulka, he was too familiar with the inconsistencies of French Catholics to be sceptical about the sincerity of the waiter's reverence as he processed with the monks and the other acolytes into the sanctuary. Watching the sandy haired priest's grave face through the open side door, Hilliard began to understand better why Sardine had refused so vehemently to co-operate any longer in the promotion of the not invariably spiritual policies of the West.

"What are *you* doing here?" Behind Hilliard and the again kneeling Wanda was standing his fourth unexpected encounter in less than an hour: Admiral Sir David Doddick. "Don't tell me you're a holy Roman too."

"No; just a visitor." In spite of what he had said to Karminski in the bus on the way to London Airport, Hilliard was mathematician enough to feel that he was meeting far too many people he knew in this monastery and its environs for their presence there together at the same time to be coincidental. Hippolyte's alone seemed above suspicion. The explanation for the Admiral's must be subversive contact with Sardine. Might it not have been the unexpected sight of Kipper among the matchfolder collector pilgrims to the Powązki military cemetery that had made Sardine turn tail and run? Might not Kipper have thought it his duty to come and have it out with Sardine? Karminski had had his doubts about the Admiral from the very beginning. And hadn't Sardine said that Caviare generally sent Catholic agents to Poland?

"Father Borowski was at Stonyhurst with my son." The Admiral tipped his chin towards the sanctuary where Sardine, helped by the other two monks, was now walking about the altar washing it with puffs of incense. "And a monastery's the best hide out I know from MacOggski. When I telephoned

Nodder about the shirts he said they weren't there any longer so I suppose a represenative of the Free World must have pinched them."

Hilliard took heart again. The Admiral's story about the shirts was grotesque enough to have the ring of truth. Sardine's schoolboy friendship with Tomato's son could account both for the priest's knowledge of English and for the Admiral's presence at Kłock. The Admiral's and the Chinese Ambassador's departure from the reception in each other's company had probably been no more than a couple of distinguished topers getting together for a nightcap.

"By the way, Arbuthnot, when are you due to pull out for England?"

"Thursday if all goes well." If the Admiral wasn't Kipper it would be useless for Hilliard to say anything about the mess he was in with Karminski.

"Lucky you! I've still to go on to Kraków and Częstochowa. Look, I wonder if I could ask you to post this letter for me when you get back. Although there's supposed to be no censorship here, with those Communist Nosey Parkers one never knows. I've no English small change on me either, but as your name's not MacOggski I don't suppose you'll mind paying for the stamp."

"A pleasure, I'm sure." But the mention of censorship had made Hilliard uneasy again. Sliding the letter into his pocket, he decided to open the envelope at the first opportunity and if the contents looked at all dubious, destroy them. He was in too much trouble with Karminski already to risk getting into more because of the Admiral.

Wanda rose from her knees to make way for the tiny procession as it came back into the sacristy.

"Father, I want you to meet my friend Arbuthnot. Not one of ours unfortunately, but his heart's in the right place."

The priest bowed. His expression showed no surprise that the Admiral should have introduced Hilliard by a name other than his own.

90

"And as he's off back to England on Thursday he's the very chap to post that letter of yours you were telling me about."

"If it's not too much bother for you, Mr. Arbuthnot, I'd be grateful." The priest pulled an envelope out of a pocket in his habit and handed it to Hilliard. "It's illegal for us to send unused stamps out of Poland and I've a friend in England who collects them."

"That's all right, Father." Although he didn't imagine that Sardine would risk entrusting a secret message to a man he knew Karminski suspected of being Whale, Hilliard wasn't going to take any chances: he would open the priest's letter when he opened the Admiral's and destroy it if it looked subversive.

"And this, Father, is Miss Zamoyska. Her newspaper was flattering enough to think I was worth interviewing."

"Miss Zamoyska and I are old friends. And now if you and Mr. Arbuthnot will excuse us I've some private business I'd like to discuss with her."

"You seem to have got what it takes all right," the Admiral said to Hilliard when Father Borowski and Wanda had gone away together. "The answer was a lemon when I asked her to come out with *me*. All right, Arbuthnot, if you can't be good be careful. And thanks for looking after that letter for me." The Admiral gave Hilliard a segment of salute and strode out into the cloister.

It wasn't difficult for Hilliard to guess the nature of the "private business" which Father Borowski was going to discuss with Wanda. Without entering into details, the priest would tell her that it was dangerous for her to associate with a man who, to his own knowledge, traveled about Poland using two names. Wanda would then tell Father Borowski what Hilliard had told her. But would the story about the suitcase and the overcoat make Father Borowski stop imagining that Hilliard was Whale and consent to help him as well as Wanda, so ludicrously suspected of being Sardine? Hilliard was so worried by these uncertainties that he almost failed to answer Hippolyte's farewell and the monks' and other acolytes' bows when they left the sacristy.

A quarter of an hour later Wanda came running back.

"Your overcoat friend's just turned up and asked to see the Prior," she said. "Father Borowski says we're to beat it while the going's good."

17

Outside the main door of the church the grey Citroën was again drawn up behind the Syrena, but Wanda's calm as she folded herself into the driving seat shamed Hilliard into controlling his panic.

"*Dzika Kaczka*, Wild Duck in English, that's how your friend's known in trade circles. Anyway Father Borowski's going to try to keep talking as long as possible so as to give us a decent start. The main thing is to prevent him finding out where we're making for—if it *is* us he's after, that is. Father Borowski says that with people like Wild Duck one never knows."

"And where *are* we making for?" Things must have worked out all right after all. The priest must have thought up a plan to save both Wanda and himself. The Syrena was already tearing along the road, but when Hilliard looked out through the back window he saw that the Citroën was still parked in front of the monastery door.

"Poznań—that's where we're making for. A friend of Father Borowski's called Anchovy lives there. But don't try to dodge the issue. Why didn't you tell me that it was Father Borowski who was Sardine?"

"How could I have? I didn't know myself until I recognized him in the sacristy."

"At least you could have told me that you knew that such a person as Sardine really existed and that you had met him. Why didn't you? Because you didn't trust me?"

"Of course not. I just didn't want to frighten you more than was necessary, that's all."

"That wouldn't have frightened me. On the contrary it would have *un*frightened me because then I should have known that there was a real Sardine for Karminski to suspect instead of only me. You've been telling me the truth about yourself, I hope. Not that it makes any difference of course. Father Borowski says that it's still my duty to help you even if you *are* Whale."

"You can set your mind at ease about that. I am no more Whale than you are Sardine."

"It's not because of the Admiral introducing you to Father Borowski as Arbuthnot that I'm asking—the Admiral's always calling people Arbuthnot, Father Borowski says. It's because knowing you truly aren't Whale will help me to be braver if we're caught. My uncle always says that the only reason he wasn't shot by the Gestapo during the Insurrection was because he never allowed them to see how frightened he was when they interrogated him. My father and my mother were not so clever."

"How terrible for you!" As he uttered the inadequate words, Hilliard was surprised to discover that in spite of his affection for her he had never thought of her as living, or not living, with parents: like Berkeleian tables and chairs, her versatile little face and its rapid declensions of mood had been snuffed out when he wasn't there to observe them. The grey Citroën, he was glad to see when he looked through the back windows again, still seemed to be non-existing outside the monastery door.

"Naturally, being the man he is, when I told Father Borowski what had happened, he wanted to give himself up to the Security Police at once, and you've no idea what a hard job I had persuading him not to. But in the end I managed to get him to see how much more important he was to Poland than I was. Even then he still kept on pointing out that it wouldn't only be me he would be saving but you as well because if he gave himself up he said that he would almost certainly be able to stop Karminski thinking you were Whale; but I said that I knew you were much too noble a person to allow him to sacrifice himself for you like that. In that case he says the only way we can both be safe is for you to take me back to England with you."

"And just how does he expect me to do that when it's highly unlikely I'll be able to get back there myself?" Hilliard realized that his outburst sounded anything but noble, but he was too angry with Wanda for having committed him like this to care.

"That's where Anchovy comes in. Anchovy's going to give us false passports. You're to be Mr. Cyprian Antrobus-Potts and I'm to be Mrs. Cyprian Antrobus-Potts *née* something French or other to explain my bad English when we land in London. The passports are real ones sent out from England and apparently Anchovy's got all the proper rubber stamps and things. The only snag he's up against is to know which signature to forge on our visas because the Polish Consulate in London keeps changing them round, but Father Borowski says that's a chance we'll just have to take. Anyway the last lot of Antrobus-Pottses seem to have got through all right."

"For heaven's sake! He doesn't call them all Antrobus-Potts, does he?"

"Of course not. That was just a manner of speaking. The last lot of Antrobus-Pottses were Pilkington-Georges. Father Borowski says he always uses double-barrelled names because they're the next best guarantee after plus fours of *vox et praeterea nihil*."

Even in the Rush-rush Hilliard had heard of the ruses of the Hush-hush. Techniques of deceit invented in hot war had no doubt been improved in cold and both their passports and the frankings on them were likely to be convincing. In any case whether he liked Father Borowski's plan or not he had to accept it: by refusing Father Borowski's offer to save her by giving himself up Wanda had made it impossible for Hilliard to leave her behind without co-operating basely with the Dysteleological Surd, quite apart from the fact that he couldn't get away alone even if he wanted to—not after the orders Karminski had said he had issued. But nobody at the airport would be on the look out for a Mr. and Mrs. Antrobus-Potts, which was just the sort of name a couple inane enough to be matchfolder collectors might be expected to possess.

"There's also the business of the V.I.P. treatment you got at the airport when you came in. But Father Borowski says that if Anchovy does a passport photograph of you in dark glasses and you wear them at Okecie and carry a stick and walk with a limp you ought to be able to get away with it all right."

"And what about you? There'll be a hue and cry after you as well, and if I know anything about Karminski, he'll have given a pretty accurate description of you to the airport authorities—a photograph too if he's been able to lay his hands on one."

"I realize that. But Father Borowski says that if I screw up my face enough and do my hair in a pony tail and dress funnily I ought to be able to get through too."

"Tickets—what about them? As you're supposed to be an Englishwoman by marriage, yours will have to be a return one. Mine's a return all right, but it's made out in the name of Hilliard which can scarcely be construed as Antrobus-Potts writ small."

"Father Borowski didn't say anything about tickets, but I expect that was because he knew Anchovy would be able to cope."

The vague verb was frightening. Had the priest had time to think things out properly? Antrobus-Pottses couldn't travel without luggage, and now that he was on the run, Hilliard couldn't go back to the Leningrad for his because Karminski would certainly be having the hotel watched. Would Anchovy be able to rustle up the sort of English-looking suitcases Antrobus-Pottses required as well as provide all the documentary paraphernalia?

Then another fear assailed Hilliard. On his arrival at Okecie his passport had been taken from him at one window and handed back to him at another a few feet further on.

Might not his name have been listed in transit so that the Harold Twinberrow Hilliard who left Poland could be proved to be a Harold Twinberrow Hilliard who had entered it? No Antrobus-Pottses had ever come in at Okecie. But perhaps Anchovy was going to make them Antrobus-Pottses who had arrived by train or bus from Moscow whither they had gone direct from London by air. For that Soviet visas, airport and police registration stamps would be required. Had Anchovy the tools for these as well? Anyway the Pilkington-Georges had got back all right. If Hilliard wanted peace of mind he would have to have the same sort of blind trust in Anchovy as laymen in baptism and surgery.

"How are you going to let your uncle know about all this?" Already they were driving back through the unsmiling dirt of Drujsk, but Bishop Berkeley was still being kind and hadn't thrown up the grey Citroën on the stretch of road behind them.

"Father Borowski's going to do that. Luckily he lives in Lublin so he can't be suspected of complicity. Father Borowski says they do terrible things to people they suspect of aiding escapes to the West."

Hilliard could well believe it. The low end now justified the low means and pity had fallen into the same disrepute as prayer. The only way to bear all the pain there was in the world these days was not to think about it. Thinking evoked the image. The reason why statesmen were able to order saturation bombing of open cities and attend victory thanksgiving services with smirks on their faces afterwards was because they themselves had never seen any of the babies catch fire.

"Poznań?" Hilliard asked. "How many kilometers is it?"

"About two hundred and fifty—say four hours on roads like these. The trouble is the paper only gave me enough petrol to get to Kłock and back and like a fool I forgot to stop and fill up at Drujsk, but with a bit of luck we ought to be able to lay our hands on some at Brodnica."

"And what if we can't?" Hilliard was becoming alarmed

again: too many things altogether seemed to have been left to chance.

"I'll just have to send out a thought to the garagist at Wrocki, that's all."

"And if there's no garagist there to receive it, what then?"

"In that case I'll send out thoughts to the garagists at Lipnica, Kowalewo and Toruń and to Wild Duck as well to think that we're on our way back to Warsaw. But if none of them work and Wild Duck's really after us we'll be caught and tortured and if we die we'll be martyrs, but I expect it'll be easier for me than for you because I'll be dying for Catholic Poland and you'll only be dying for stocks and shares."

He saw then that she was making fun of him, but it was relief, not resentment, that he felt.

Night was already beginning to fall and the candles round another new grave glowed on a field that had been turned dark blue like a sea. Brodnica however was as grimy as Drujsk and there were the same shabby people walking its despairing streets. In a cul-de-sac to which one of these down-at-heel ghosts directed Wanda, a mechanic with an oil-stained face poured petrol into the Syrena's tank out of tins. When Hilliard offered to pay Wanda wouldn't allow him to and, from the smile she gave the mechanic as she pressed notes into his hands, Hilliard guessed that the purchase had been a black market one.

"We ought to be all right now," Wanda said as she did a deft piece of backing. "Sixty liters the tank holds and that's more than enough to get us to Poznań and back to Warsaw when Anchovy's fixed us up with our false passports and things which Father Borowski says ought to be by Wednesday morning at the latest."

That was another thing the priest seemed to have overlooked. The Syrena as well as Wanda was going to be missed by *Polska Prawda* on Monday morning and the traffic police all over Poland would be ordered to be on the look out for it.

Unless Anchovy was able to provide them with false number plates and car papers, the only safe way for them to go back to Warsaw would be by train.

But the continued absence of following lights after they had left Brodnica began to soothe Hilliard with the ignoble hope that it was Father Borowski's activities and not his own and Wanda's that Wild Duck had called at the monastery to investigate. The dark blue night enveloped them like a stained glass window and the road was a golden wake unrolled in reverse in front of their headlamps. The trees sank as gently back into the darkness as they had emerged from it and Hilliard almost forgot his fears in the thrill of being alone in this friendly blotted out world with Wanda.

Then suddenly the engine began to sputter. The gold wash stopped flowing and became a motionless pool. Each time Wanda tried the starter there was a gripless whirring which subsided as soon as she let go of the ignition key.

"Do you know anything about cars, Professor Hilliard, because I don't?"

"Less than nothing, I'm afraid." Even when he had been at school, Hilliard had despised engineering and regarded it, like bookkeeping, as a subject for dull boys with no talent for syntax. Hollow with fright, he now saw how wrong he had been: bolts, screws, pressures, pistons and valves were what wagged the dog's tail nowadays and even David Hume would have been unable to doubt their existence had not the bolts, screws, pressures, pistons and valves not been there to be proved illusory.

"Then the only thing to do is to pray to St. Christopher."

"Sparking plugs—do you think it could be sparking plugs?" Hilliard remembered having heard that sparking plugs required cleaning from time to time. "Let's have a look, shall we?"

But when, with Wanda's help, he lifted up the hood he was no more capable of distinguishing sparking plugs from cylinders than infinitives from nouns in a paragraph of Polish prose.

"Sorry," he said. "I can't make head or tail of it and I daren't risk fiddling."

"Then what about my walking back to Brodnica? It can't be more than six or seven kilometers and they'll probably have some sort of repair wagon in that garage place."

"If anybody's doing any walking back I'm the person that's going to do it. I'll be able to make the chap understand what's happened by signs all right. The only thing is, it means leaving you to deal with Wild Duck alone if he turns up while I'm away."

"He's scarcely likely to do that now. Either he must have lost track of us or Father Borowski's sent him chasing back to Warsaw. But don't let's do anything rash. After all, there's still the odd chance that it may only be flooding. Anyway I'll try the starter again in ten minutes or so and see."

Back in the darkness of the car again the indistinct hover of her face tempted him. Only by remembering the trouble other elderly men had got themselves into through lack of self-control was Hilliard able to restrain himself from an attempt at a caress. Their hand holding at Drujsk had been only pretence and he had no idea how a girl with Wanda's religious temperament would react to what she might very well interpret as a prelude to rape. "RECTOR WAVES SEX FLAG AT SOPRANO IN CHOIR LOFT"; recalling the ribaldry the caption had caused in the common room, Hilliard decided that he would rather be tortured by Karminski than have a headline like that about himself appear in the London *Bugle*.

"Flooding! What did I tell you?" The engine had started as soon as Wanda had turned the key.

But on the outskirts of Kowalewo the engine began to sputter again and before they reached Toruń they had broken down three times. In Toruń, Wanda made straight for a garage. The garage had a neon sign above the door which said WARSZTAT SAMOCHODOWY. While Wanda was explaining their troubles to the mechanic, Hilliard sat thinking how difficult it must be to learn a language that called a garage a *Warsztat Samochodowy*.

"Water in the petrol, he says. That fellow in Brodnica of course. Anyway it's no use crying over spilt milk. He says it'll take at least an hour to drain the tank so let's go and see if we can get something to eat."

There was a hotel almost next door to the *Warsztat Samochodowy*. The dining room was as dour as the one in Drujsk, but when the dilapidated waiter switched on their table lamp Wanda's green hat lit up the gloom and made it glow like the shadows on a Zurbarán.

"*Hop siup!*" Hilliard raised his yellow tulip of Zubrowka to Wanda's. "But ought *you* to be drinking? I thought you said it was twenty-four hours without, when you were driving."

"*Hop siup!* There's not much danger of running into the police at this time of night and after all that waiting about on the road I need something to warm me up."

"I'm sure you do."

"Father Borowski says that when we get to England I'll probably have to stay with you until the British Government grants me political asylum and I can look for some sort of job. I hope your wife won't object. She'll understand it's only your mind I'm in love with, won't she?"

"But perhaps not that it's only your mind that *I'm* in love with." Hilliard was so hurt by her frankness that he almost forgot that they were by no means either of them out of danger yet. When he had been young it had been his knowledge of Spinoza he had wanted girls to admire, now it was the middle-aged face in front of it.

"Don't worry about that. She'll soon realize she's nothing to be afraid of. The Doctors of the Church say that watching a girl eat her breakfast morning after morning is the best way to keep a married man from committing adultery with her in his heart."

It was only the thoughts which they weren't having that

people couldn't hide. Hilliard knew that Charlotte never thought about philosophy, but Charlotte didn't know how often Hilliard thought about girls. But hankering after a bright waterproof in a bus queue was one thing and having the girl you were in love with to stay in your house another. Even so, a man who had stood up to Karminski alias Bekas or Snipe wasn't going to put up with any nonsense from Charlotte. Charlotte would have to be made to realize that she was no longer dealing with a weakling who took unused tickets to the *Messiah* lying down. Charlotte would have to be made to see the image.

"And what's more you're not really in love with me. You're lonely, that's all."

What else but lonely could a man be with a wife who talked about "you and your deep books"? His friends, who were they? The colleagues he had pretended to like for fifteen years for fear of finding out that they had been only pretending to like him?

"Everybody's lonely, you know," Wanda went on as she tossed back her second Zubrowka. "The only cure for loneliness is death."

"Not even that apparently:

'Oh! Death will find me, long before I tire
Of watching you; and swing me suddenly
Into the shade and loneliness and mire
Of the last land!'"

But from the eagerness with which Wanda greeted the waiter as he arrived with the next course Hilliard gathered that his translation of Rupert Brooke into French had not been very successful.

Whatever the Doctors of the Church had said, Charlotte was capable of taking the bit between her teeth and turning Wanda out of the house long before the statutory sequence of breakfasts had been completed. If she did, Hilliard would take the bit between *his* teeth and leave with Wanda. Pious or not,

Wanda would then have to let him live with her. Would she find it so difficult? Had she really meant what she had said about loving him only in her heart? Hadn't the pressure of her hand on his in the dining room at Drujsk been a little too warm to have been only pretending? Mightn't the pretending have been pretending to pretend? If it had, why should he scruple to take what she offered him? Young bodies could uplift old bodies as well as degrade them. Hilliard was pretty sure Bilsborrow wasn't external-examining at Imperial College every time he went up to London. Lust after all was only biology. "$βίος$" he whispered softly across the table at her lick of red hair but even as he heard the rustle of the grave Greek word he knew that his argument was a false one. Biology was for the young. It was so exclusively for the young that if he ran away with Wanda he would have to resign his chair and try to earn his living with writing. Sex and adventure were the money spinners, Catacomb had said. *The Gorilla and the Nymphet in the Sputnik* by Cyprian Antrobus-Potts? He'd rather clean windows at Catacomb and Priddle's than sink as low.

"Hop siup, Haroldek!" Wanda grinned blearily at Hilliard as she raised her third glass of Zubrowka. There was no longer any room for surmise: St. Catherine of Siena was tiddly.

"Hop siup, Wanda!"

" 'Hop siup, Wandzia!' you should say. *Wandzia's* the diminutive of Wanda." Snowflakes began to fall behind the window on the Zurbarán and soon they were draping Wanda like a mantilla.

"This isn't going to make things any easier for us, is it?" Hilliard unharnessed Wanda from the cataract of lace by making her turn round and look at it.

"On the contrary. But if we do without coffee and leave right away we ought to be able to make Poznań before the roads are blocked. I'd ask for the bill though if I were you: Karminski might give us an extra tweak or two with the red hot pincers if he found out we'd left without paying." From the smile that accompanied the pat she gave his shoulder as she rose and left him, Hilliard knew that she was back at her joking again.

When it was Hilliard's turn to go to the Tualeta instead of the now almost platitudinous MĘSKI and DAMSKI he found doors labeled DLA PANOW and DLA PAŃ. After a little hesitation he entered DLA PAŃ. As he was on the point of leaving again he remembered the letters which the Admiral and Father Borowski had given him to post in England and realized that he would never find a more suitable place for reading them and discarding their contents if these were subversive. Father Borowski's letter was addressed to:

REV ALOYSIUS GILHOOLEY, S.J.
CHURCH OF THE SACRED HEART,
LAURISTON STREET,
EDINBURGH.

Using the method he employed at home when wanting to add a postscript to a letter already sealed and stamped, Hilliard opened the envelope by rolling the point of his Biro under the flap. Inside there were five or six squares of unused Polish stamps of various denominations. There was no accompanying letter, Hilliard licked the flap down and put the letter back in his pocket.

The Admiral's letter was addressed to:

Personal
REAR-ADMIRAL SIR PERCY CHILDERSTONE, K.C.B.,
DIRECTOR OF NAVAL INTELLIGENCE,
THE ADMIRALTY,
WHITEHALL,
LONDON, S.W.1.

Doubt there could no longer be: Kipper, Kedgeree or Finnan Haddock, the Admiral *was* an agent, and for Hilliard to risk being caught carrying what was obviously one of his reports to Headquarters would be madness. Afraid to acquaint himself with a message whose matter could only make him more frightened than he was already, Hilliard was about to tear the letter up unopened when somebody began to hammer imperatively on the lavatory door behind him.

Convinced that the knocker must be Wild Duck, Hilliard threw the envelope into the water closet and pulled the plug; but when the churning was over, the letter was still lying at the bottom of the pan. Fishing the dripping envelope out again he stuffed it into his pocket, opened the door and found himself facing the grubby waiter who had served them in the dining room.

"Damski nie Męski," the waiter said with a glare and shot into DLA PANÓW.

Hilliard's amusement at his mistake lasted until they were stopped by three policemen outside Toruń. At first his only fear was that they would smell the alcohol in Wanda's breath, but when Wanda told him that one of the policemen wanted to see his passport he realized that the check was something quite different from routine traffic control. He had just time to slip the Admiral's letter down the window well before he and Wanda were both handcuffed, dragged from their seats and pushed into the back of the car.

18

One of the policemen took Wanda's seat at the wheel, turned the car and drove it back towards Toruń. Another sat beside him with his face screwed round to watch Hilliard and Wanda so that it looked as though he were wearing his uniform the wrong way round. The third policeman rode in front of the car on a motorcycle with an empty sidecar. The headlamps of the car and the motorcycle kept creating snowy stretches of road for them to drive along and fields on either side even whiter than the road. There was snow on the trees as well now and the road and the fields and the trees all kept on coming up new and white together in the light of the headlamps.

"Cisza!" the policeman sitting beside the driver bawled when Hilliard tried to ask Wanda if she had been informed why they had been arrested, and scowled so fiercely that Hilliard was sure that he would be beaten up if he persisted.

But as soon as they had passed through Toruń without stopping Hilliard knew that their arrest had nothing to do with Wanda's drinking. Wild Duck had been too clever for them. Wild Duck had had ample opportunity to note down the Syrena's number and instead of following whatever false trail Father Borowski might have given him, had alerted all the road police. It was to Warsaw that they were returning, to Warsaw and to Karminski. The Antrobus-Pottses had died before they had been born.

Perilous as their plight had been before, it was now little short of catastrophic. Karminski was almost certainly aware of Caviare's plan to use Poland's Catholicity to strengthen the defences of the West and their visit to the monks at Kłock must have been final proof for him that Hilliard was Whale and that Wanda was Sardine. As soon as they got back to Warsaw they would be interrogated separately and if their stories differed they would both be lost.

As far as Hilliard could foresee there were four questions which Karminski was bound to ask each of them:

Was Hilliard Whale?

Was Wanda Sardine?

Why had they been visiting the monastery at Kłock?

Why had they been driving so late at night towards Poznań instead of returning to Warsaw?

Wanda would say that Hilliard wasn't Whale. Hilliard would say that Hilliard wasn't Whale. Wanda would say that Wanda wasn't Sardine. Hilliard would say that Wanda wasn't Sardine. But what would Wanda's answer be if Karminski asked her whether Hilliard had told her that Karminski suspected him of being Whale and herself of being Sardine? Most likely, because concealment would seem proof of Hilliard's guilty conscience, that he had. Of one thing however Hilliard was sure: even if threatened with torture, even if tortured, Wanda would never try to clear herself by telling Karminski that it was Father Borowski who was Sardine. Could Hilliard be as confident about himself? Would a man who had bumsucked Royal Army Pay Corps lance corporals be able to stand up to the tweezers and the branding irons. Would he be any better at bravery than the other smooth men who had skulked out the war in chairborne jobs and who now directed the Establishment with the genial confidence of those who knew they could no longer be put to the test?

Would he be able to stand up to the thought of Wanda standing up to the tweezers and the branding irons? Would Wanda be able to stand up to the thought of Hilliard standing up to the tweezers and the branding irons? Therein lay his only hope of escape with nobility: that he would denounce Father Borowski to save Wanda or, better still, that Wanda would denounce him to save Hilliard.

What would be Wanda's answer when Karminski asked her why she and Hilliard had been visiting the monastery at Kłock? As near the truth as possible obviously: that she had wanted to introduce Hilliard to the monks because of her admiration for their attempt to reconcile Catholic theology with Marxist economics.

But what reason would she give for their making so late at night for Poznań instead of returning to Warsaw? Repeating her tactic in the hotel restaurant at Drujsk and remembering that Wild Duck had seen them holding hands there, she would almost certainly say that they were lovers seeking privacy in a town where neither of them was known.

To convey to her that this would be his answer too and to impress the still vigilant policeman with their intimacy, Hilliard dumped his handcuffed wrists on top of Wanda's and left them lying in her lap beside hers. But even the warmth of her palms upturned to greet his couldn't stop the dialectic that went thumping on and on in his brain like a paddle steamer. The policeman would tell Karminski about their holding hands in the car and Wild Duck would tell him about their holding hands in the restaurant. But would Karminski attach any importance to the information? Mightn't Karminski be clever enough to realize that it was all a put up job or man of the world enough to conclude that fellow conspirators could fall in love with each other as easily as tennis players or match-folder collectors? As they ran on through bridal mile after bridal mile of cotton wool world Hilliard became more and more thankful that he had at least managed to get rid of the Admiral's letter.

Shortly before they reached the outskirts of Warsaw the motorcycle and sidecar stopped and the Syrena drew up close behind. Wanda was the first to be blindfolded. As the black band was whipped round her eyes she pummeled Hilliard's hands so vigorously that he knew she must be sending out a thought to him, and before he had been blindfolded himself he had guessed what it was: that just as she was not going to betray Father Borowski to save him so he must not betray Father Borowski to save her. Wanda wasn't going to betray Father Borowski because Father Borowski was the image of Poland. England had no image these days and that was what was going to make heroism so much harder for Hilliard than for Wanda. Emboldened by the blotting out of the policeman's scowl, Hilliard tried to whisper to Wanda that he understood, but as soon as his lips began to move the shout of *"Cisza!"* came and the most he could do to communicate his assent was to increase the pressure of his hands on hers.

Ten minutes or so later the car stopped again and Wanda and Hilliard were ordered to get out. Hilliard's arms were seized and he was led from the gentle pat of snowflakes into a smell of dust and cold walls. The policeman said a word which Hilliard didn't understand and a long descent of stairs began. Remembering what he had read about what went on in secret police basements in Communist countries, Hilliard controlled his terror only by his determination not to show up as a coward in front of Wanda.

But when the bandage was removed from his eyes he found that Wanda and her escort had vanished and that he was alone with his policeman in a pistache-green room whose only furniture was a few chairs and a desk in front of which the policeman stood holding him by the arm. Above the desk hung an unlighted lantern, and according to the angle at which Hilliard held his head the shadows thrown on the lantern by the lamps on the walls formed the figure of an old man or a girl sitting with her hands clasped round her knees. The old man had changed into the girl and back again six or seven times before an almost invisible door in the wall behind the desk opened and Karminski and Wild Duck came in. Karminski sat down at the desk looking as though he were finding it difficult to keep his head steady because of all the syllogisms crashing about like boulders inside it and Wild Duck remained standing beside him wearing a grin as jagged as a tear in a sardine tin. When the policeman had made his report, he un-handcuffed Hilliard, saluted and went out through the door by which he had entered with Hilliard.

"How lucky it was that it was today which I chose to go and tell these monks about the extra taxes that the Government is going to impose upon them," Wild Duck said to Hilliard and then walked briskly out again through the door behind the desk.

"Professor Hilliard," Karminski said, "I am going to give you one last chance to play ball with me. Why have you been visiting a seditious monastery in the company of Miss Zamoyska? Surely the Jasna Góra in Częstochowa would have been a more suitable beauty spot for a girl reporter from *Polska Prawda* to take a visiting professor of philosophy?"

"Professors of philosophy are interested in philosophy more than in beauty spots. I wanted to meet the monks at Kłock because of what Miss Zamoyska had told me about their attempt to reconcile Christianity with Marxism. A busman's holiday, in other words."

"Fine ham, Professor Hilliard! If that was your only reason for going to see the monks why did one of them give you a letter to post for him when you got back to England?"

Sardine had said that even cemetery walls had ears in Poland. The same must be true of sacristies. Either one of the monks or one of the acolytes had been suborned by Karminski. As Hilliard reached this conclusion the telephone bell rang and while Karminski was answering Hilliard prepared his reply. If he showed any reluctance to hand over Father Borowski's envelope Karminski would conclude that Hilliard either knew or imagined that there was a subversive message inside it. Letting the priest in for a reprimand for sending unused postage stamps out of Poland was preferable by far to having Karminski begin to suspect him of being Sardine. Sure that Wanda would agree, Hilliard pulled the envelope which Father Borowski had given him out of his pocket and laid it on the desk.

"If that's all that's biting you," he said when Karminski had replaced the receiver.

Karminski smiled contemptuously as he read the address, but examined the back of the envelope for so long and so attentively that Hilliard began to be afraid lest he had noticed that it had been opened and resealed. Finally however Karminski detached the flap the same way as Hilliard had done, by inserting the point of a pen at the top and running it down both sides.

"Stamps! Next thing we'll be hearing is that the Pope collects matchfolders." Switching on a lamp with a green shade like Wanda's funny hat, Karminski inspected the stamps back and front before replacing them in the envelope. "Did it occur to you to ask his reverence why he couldn't post the stamps himself?"

"I didn't require to: he told me of his own accord. He said that it was against the law to send unused stamps out of Poland."

"Precisely. And for that reason the stamps will have to be confiscated." Karminski slid the envelope into a compartment of his wallet. "And now, Professor Hilliard, perhaps you will be kind enough to show me the other letter which you were given to post in England."

"The priest gave me no other letter to post in England."

"I am aware of that. It is the letter which the Admiral gave you to post for him in England that I wish to see."

"Your spy must have been using his eyes badly: the Admiral gave me no letter to post for him in England or anywhere else." This time Hilliard was pretty sure that Karminski was bluffing. Only Wanda had been in the sacristy when the Admiral had handed over his letter, and the risk of her talking about it under interrogation was so slight as to be negligible.

"Professor Hilliard, when we were on that bus in England together you told me that you did not know the Admiral. Later I found out that not only did you know him, but that you knew him well enough to go to a reception at the British Embassy in his company and to meet him secretly in the Powązki military cemetery. If you lied to me about not knowing the Admiral why should you not also lie to me about the letter which he gave you to post for him when you returned to England?"

"I thought we'd been through all that already. I didn't meet the Admiral secretly in the Powązki cemetery. I ran into him there by chance just as it was by chance that I happened to be on hand when he wanted somebody to carry MacOgg's shirts to the British Embassy for him."

"And it was also by chance that you ran into him in the sacristy of the monastery at Kłock where it was also by chance that he gave you a letter to post for him in England?" Karminski's face was as blank as the wall of a brewery.

"The Admiral gave me no letter to post for him in England." Reiteration, after all, was a two-edged sword. If Karminski could hope to brainwash Hilliard into saying that the Admiral *had* given him a letter to post in England, might not Hilliard hope to brainwash Karminski into thinking that the Admiral had *not* given him a letter to post in England? The Admiral had been standing nowhere near the door giving on to the sanctuary when he had handed over the letter and the suborned monk or acolyte could not possibly have seen him doing so.

"You cross your heart and hope to die?"

"I cross my heart and hope to die."

"You are dead sure?"

"I am dead sure."

"In that case I shall have to make deader sure." Karminski took up the telephone and spoke a sentence or two in Polish.

A few seconds later two men with treacherous eyes as small as aspirin tablets came in. Without a word of instruction from Karminski they snatched Hilliard's wallet, passport and air ticket folder out of his pocket and laid them on the desk for Karminski to examine. When they had gone through Hilliard's other pockets they tore off his jacket, pulled the sleeves inside out and felt all the lining. They ripped off his waistcoat and did the same thing with it. Then they made him sit down and take off his shoes and socks. After they had looked inside these and tugged his toes apart they stripped him completely and thrust a paper knife up his anus so roughly that Hilliard squealed. By the time the men had finished with him and left and Karminski told him that he could dress again, Hilliard was on the verge of blubbering.

For he knew that as yet he was only on the outer boulevards of the Dysteleological Surd and that much worse was to follow. Even if Karminski was now satisfied that the Admiral hadn't given Hilliard any letter to post in England, there was still the hurdle of Sardine to get over. If Wanda wasn't Sardine and Hilliard wasn't Whale what had they been doing on the road to Poznań together so long after dark? Would Karminski accept the explanation that they were lovers? Karminski's dead pan face as he handed Hilliard back his belongings didn't suggest that Karminski would. If Hilliard had squealed at the thrust of a paper knife how was he going to stand up to torture? Intellectuals had generally to pay for plenitude of brain by defect of body. Just as James Joyce would have been grateful for an Irish laborer's eyes, so it looked as though Hilliard might soon be willing to exchange his erudition for a docker's kidneys. Kicking was the way it generally began, they said, kicking with a gramophone or a wireless turned on full blast to drown the screaming.

"How did you get rid of the letter, Professor Hilliard? By swallowing it? We know it's not in the car because we've searched it." Karminski was sitting so still that he looked like a photograph of himself.

"Why should you think that? I didn't try to get rid of the priest's letter, did I?" Had the Admiral by any chance mentioned his own letter when he had suggested to Father Borowski that Hilliard should post his? Hilliard didn't think so but wished he could be sure.

113

"There was no need for you to get rid of the priest's letter. The priest had told you that there were only unused Polish stamps inside. You had no reason to believe that it contained any reference to intrigue."

"I had even less reason for believing that a letter which never existed contained any reference to intrigue. Use your common sense, Mr. Karminski. Why should the Admiral have given me a letter to post in England when he could perfectly well have posted it for himself when he got back?" The Admiral *must* have mentioned his own letter when suggesting that Hilliard should post Father Borowski's. Nothing else could account for Karminski's insistence.

"No doubt because the letter is important and the Admiral has still a lot of other business to attend to before he leaves Poland. Anyway what is a man like the Admiral doing in a monastery? Religion would scarcely seem to be his cup of tea."

"The strangest sort of people repent sometimes and the Admiral's just about the right age for promising to give up Since October girls for ever for a month." Although far from being amused by his own joke, Hilliard managed to scratch up a sketchy grin.

"Come off it, Professor Hilliard. The Admiral gave you a letter to post for him in England and I want to know what you have done with it."

"The Admiral gave me no letter, I tell you. And if he had do you think I'd have been such a fool as to accept it? I was in enough trouble with you as it was already, wasn't I? And as I'm not going to be allowed to return to England until I confirm that Miss Zamoyska's some absurd person called Sardine what hope could I have had of being able to post it?"

" 'Hope springs eternal in the human breast,' as your poet Pope says. What hope had you of being able to post the priest's letter?"

"Stamps aren't like letters; stamps can wait."

"So it would seem. Professor Hilliard, just what were you

and your lady friend doing outside Toruń at such a tardy hour of the night?"

"Why does anyone drive anywhere with pretty girls at tardy hours of the night?" Hilliard stretched his lips into what he hoped looked like a leer.

"So although Miss Zamoyska is little more than a schoolgirl and too young to be involved in cloak and dagger business she is not too young to be the victim of a fate worse than death?"

"Platonic friendships with intellectual young women often develop into emotional ones when the parties concerned have intellectual interests in common."

"But why outside Toruń, Professor Hilliard? Toruń's not on the direct road from Kłock to Warsaw."

"It wasn't Warsaw we were making for; it was Poznań." As soon as the name was out of his mouth Hilliard realized that he had been too communicative: Karminski who knew so much might have very well heard rumors about Anchovy and the Pilkington-Georges.

"Why Poznań? Poznań's a stale and stodgy city. Why did neither you nor Miss Zamoyska think of Międzyzdrój and the sad sea waves?"

"I don't know. I left the thinking to Miss Zamoyska. She knows Poland; I don't."

"What was wrong with inviting her up to your room at the Leningrad?"

"Lots. For one thing I wasn't sure if I'd be able to get past the floor girl and there'd also have been the danger of bumping into MacOgg in the corridor."

"And what about the danger of bumping into the Admiral in the corridor? Or would you not have minded about him?"

"The Admiral was no longer at the Leningrad. The Admiral was at the monastery."

"So you admit that before you left for the monastery with Miss Zamoyska you knew that you were going to meet the Admiral there?"

"On the contrary nobody could have been more surprised than I was when I ran into him there."

"In that case why did you not say that one of your reasons for not taking Miss Zamoyska up to your room at the Leningrad was because you were afraid of bumping into MacOgg and/or the Admiral in the corridor?"

"Because when I made the remark I had already met the Admiral at the monastery and knew that he was staying there and consequently wouldn't be available for being bumped into in corridors at the Leningrad. In other words I was expressing my prudence in the light of previous information."

"I suggest that you were expressing your prudence in the light of information even more previous than that. I suggest that your meeting with the Admiral at Kłock was prearranged between you when you met in the Powązki military cemetery and was contrived for the same reason: because both of you knew that I was watching your contacts at the Leningrad. Indeed I am not so sure that it was not your intention to run into him by chance in Poznań. Why could you not have taken Miss Zamoyska to some other hotel in Warsaw? There are no MacOggs to be bumped into in the corridors of the Bristol or the Grand."

"Because Miss Zamoyska happens to be very well known in Warsaw and I didn't want to run the slightest risk of compromising her."

"Tell that to the Royal Marines! Once and for all, Whale, what have you done with the letter which the Admiral gave you to post in England?"

"The Admiral gave me no letter to post in England and once and for all, Bekas, I am not Whale."

"And once and for all, Professor Hilliard, if you are not Whale how do you know that I am Bekas?" But Hilliard had already realized that he had made the irretrievable mistake.

"Your employers would appear to have trained you very badly," Karminski went on after a triumphant display of fretsaw teeth. "First of all you allow yourself to be caught attempting to rifle my suitcase at London Airport. Then you purloin my friend's overcoat at Schönefeld in order to examine the contents of his pockets and are caught with it red-handed on your back coming out of the lavatory. You reveal a knowledge of foreign languages possessed only by Britons who work for M.I.5. You manifest a familiarity with the stupid conduct of German generals in the last war which could not have been acquired by anyone who had performed his military service in the Royal Army Pay Corps as you pretended to me that *you* had. You flaunt yourself at a reception at the British Embassy in the company of your confederate. And to crown everything you call me by a name which you could not possibly have known unless you were the British agent you have denied all along that you were."

Hilliard stared dismally up at the girl's knees changing back into the old man's waistcoat on the lantern. He was in a cleft stick: to tell Karminski how he had discovered that Karminski was Bekas would mean betraying Father Borowski; not to betray Father Borowski would mean involving Wanda in the appalling consequences of his *gaffe*.

"I warn you, Professor Hilliard, that in order to carry out the duties of my office I have sometimes to be ruthless. I hope that you will spare me the necessity of being so with you. For the last time, what have you done with the Admiral's letter?"

If he hadn't been handcuffed and if the policeman sitting beside the driver hadn't been watching him so intently Hilliard would have said that he had thrown it out of the car window at some indeterminate point on the journey back to Warsaw: a letter so discarded would now be buried beneath inches of snow and its disappearance when the thaw came could be attributed to floods or gales. To say that he had thrown it out of the window *before* he had been handcuffed would be useless because the point outside Toruń where they had been arrested would certainly have been searched by now. To say that he had swallowed it would be of equally little avail: there were classic methods for recovering documents disposed

117

of in this way and their discomfort would be benign in comparison with the retribution which would follow the revelation of his lie.

"I am still willing to compromise with you," Karminski continued. "All that I ask is to be given the opportunity of acquainting myself with what the Admiral has written. If your means of getting rid of the letter has not destroyed its appearance the letter will be returned to you and you will be allowed to go back to England and post it just as though nothing had happened. Nobody shall ever know that you have shown me the letter and your dollars and pounds will also be restored to you."

Up to now Hilliard had always suspected that he was not a very brave man and that if confronted by a choice between extreme pain and its avoidance his convictions would quickly yield to his convenience. He was surprised to find that he was not as ignoble as he had imagined. The address on the Admiral's letter had made it a hundred-percent certain that the Admiral was the secret agent Hilliard was not. If Hilliard allowed Karminski to read the letter Hilliard would be guilty of treason. And even if Karminski kept his word and nobody ever heard of their shameful pact Hilliard would know for the rest of his life that he had purchased his safety at the cost of a diminution in his compatriots' security.

"If it is the fate of your confederates which is worrying you I think that I can put your mind at rest. The Admiral will be allowed to remain unmolested and no steps will be taken to counteract his intrigues until he has left Poland. The charges against Miss Zamoyska will also be dismissed. I shall do no more than warn her of the danger of consorting with the enemies of her country and as long as she obeys this counsel she will have nothing to fear from either myself or my colleagues."

Wanda—the name unfurled in Hilliard's mind like a flag. Wanda was the inspiration, Wanda was the image. Export balances could not compete with her dedicated face and haphazard hair. The Admiral too was not a statistic; the Admiral too Hilliard had seen close up.

"You are wondering perhaps what guarantee I can give you that I shall keep my word. The answer is that I can give you none. Even when you have taken off safe and sound in your crate from Okecie you will still have no means of knowing that I shall not arrest Miss Zamoyska and the Admiral as soon as you have gone. But at least you will have the comfort of knowing that you have done everything in your power to secure their safety as well as your own. Whereas if you do not tell me what you have done with the Admiral's letter you will have the sure and certain knowledge that you have been responsible for the disasters which will overwhelm them as ineluctably as they will overwhelm yourself."

It did not take Hilliard long to see that Karminski's argument was a sound one. By refusing to tell Karminski where he had hidden the Admiral's letter he would be condemning Wanda and the Admiral to the torture chamber along with himself; by allowing Karminski to read it he could at least hope to save all three of them. His duty to Wanda and the Admiral was a concentrated one, moored to his ability to imagine their faces and their limbs contorted with pain; his duty to his country a skimmy allegiance to a featureless mob of televiewers.

So, after watching the old man's waistcoat turn back into the girl's knees again, he said:

"Your policemen aren't very hot, are they? Ask them why they haven't looked in the right hand front window well of the car."

"You are right. My policemen do not seem to have been as clever as they ought to have been. Anyway I am glad that you have been sensible at last. It is foolish to be a martyr for the wrong cause." Karminski spoke abruptly and, Hilliard thought, angrily in Polish into the telephone and then sat looking at Hilliard with a forked smile. Hilliard wondered how much Karminski was despising him. If the roles had been reversed neither torture nor threat of torture would have made Karminski give in, of that Hilliard was sure.

A few minutes later one of the shifty-eyed plainclothes policemen who had searched Hilliard brought in the Admiral's letter and handed it to Karminski. Although he could see that the envelope still looked soggy, Hilliard determined to say nothing about his attempt to get rid of it in DLA PAŃ at Toruń: unless they were in immediate danger, real agents did not attempt to destroy secret messages before they had memorized them, and if Karminski were given any cause for doubting the importance of the Admiral's letter, he might be tempted to go back on his bargain.

"Snow seems to have been getting in under the window," Karminski said when he had examined the envelope. "Luckily not badly enough to blur the address which appears to be an interesting one."

To Hilliard's surprise Karminski didn't open the letter as he had opened Father Borowski's. Instead, he returned it to the plainclothes policeman who took it away again and brought it back a few minutes later with the flap unstuck. The policeman remained in the room while Karminski was reading the letter. There was no writing on the side turned towards Hilliard and the notepaper was too thick for him to try to decipher the words on the other side in obverse.

"One lives and one learns, Professor Hilliard." Karminski replaced the letter in the envelope which he handed to the policeman who took it away again. "There is no need for you to look so hot and bothered. He has only gone to gum the envelope down properly again so that there will be no danger of the Director of Naval Intelligence noticing that it has been opened and smelling a rat."

"I understand." Now that Hilliard knew himself to be safe, shame had succeeded fear, and even the reflection that he had saved Wanda's and the Admiral's skins as well as his own failed to console him. Karminski's smirk showed that he had learned something important. Recalling with dismay his own interpretation of Karminski's interest in the Admiral's visit to the Chinese Embassy, Hilliard wondered if the letter might not have contained the blueprint for a doublecross.

"You are now of course at liberty to leave Poland. Indeed you are so much at liberty to leave Poland that I prefer that you should do so first thing tomorrow morning. There is a Lot plane which takes off from Okecie at nine o'clock, and I shall see that a seat on it is reserved for you. So that there will be no risk of your missing it, I shall call for you with a car at your hotel at half-past eight, but as your dollars and pounds are not inscribed on it I shall not return them to you until you have passed through the customs barrier. Even I cannot play ducks and drakes with the regulations of the Narodowy Bank Polski." The stilted sentences were rasped out through the steel teeth as though played from a tape recording.

"Not to put too fine a point on it you're expelling me?"

"Although I have been generous I must still be prudent. I should expel the Admiral as well if I could do so without revealing our compact. I shall however watch him very carefully during the remainder of his sojourn here and as soon as he has departed, all his contacts will be interrogated and he, like yourself, will never be allowed to return to Poland. In the meantime Miss Zamoyska goes as free as the air. You will find her waiting for you outside in the car. And should you wish to say tender goodbys to her in your room at the Leningrad I think that you will find that a hundred zlotys to the floor girl will enable you to do so without a blush of shame—provided of course that you do not happen to bump into Mr. MacOgg in the corridor."

When the plainclothes policeman came back with the letter, Karminski told him to give it to Hilliard. The flap was as smooth as if it had never been opened and the address, although blotched, could still be read. As he slid the letter back into his pocket, Hilliard understood how Charlotte must have felt when she had shown him those two unused tickets for the *Messiah*.

19

Before he was led up the long staircase, Hilliard was handcuffed and blindfolded again. Outside, the snow was still falling and Hilliard could hear its silence. As soon as he had been pushed into the back of the car, other handcuffs clinked down on top of his and he knew from the insistent pressure of soft fingers that he was being warned not to talk. The car started off with a jerk and each time it turned a corner it did so so sharply that the handcuffs made a noise like a carelessly carried tea tray. When the car stopped at last, the policeman who had been driving came round and freed Wanda's and Hilliard's hands and eyes. Then he walked away rapidly and was rubbed out by the snow.

"Ludwika Krzywickiego, that's where we are," Wanda said when she had peered out through the flake draped window. "We'd better get well back into town before we start talking."

Moving into the front seat to sit beside her, Hilliard was relieved to see that neither the outside nor the inside of the door had a gash in it. The letter couldn't have fallen as deeply down the well as he had feared and the policeman must have been able to extract it with a knife or a wire. Unless the policeman had told Wild Duck or whoever it had been who had interrogated Wanda about Hilliard's bargain with Karminski there was still a good chance that Hilliard would be able to conceal his treachery. But how otherwise was he going to explain their release? Hilliard was so worried about this that it was only when Wanda drew his attention to it that he noticed the improbable Christmas card beauty of the Plac Zbawiciela.

Wanda didn't speak until she had pulled up behind a long

line of snow covered cars strung out opposite the Leningrad like a goods train waiting to be shunted.

"You got the thought I sent out to tell you what Wild Duck's telephone call to Karminski was about, I hope?"

"I'm afraid I didn't." So it had been Wild Duck who had been on the other end of the line while he had been making up his mind to show Karminski Father Borowski's letter. Hilliard wondered why he hadn't thought of that.

"But at least you managed to guess what the call was about, didn't you?"

"How could I when I don't speak Polish?"

"Don't be silly—I know that. What I meant was that Karminski might have said Dzika Kaczka several times over and then you'd have tumbled to it. Anyway what I was trying to tell you was that I'd told Wild Duck that whoever had informed him that it was a priest who'd given you a letter to post in England must have been mistaken because I'd seen with my own eyes that it was Admiral Sir David Doddick."

Why on earth had he ever told Wanda that stupid lie about his missing bath plug having been replaced in response to her telepathy? Stefan Zweig had been right: pity always prepared trouble for its practitioners. The Admiral *hadn't* mentioned his own letter when he had suggested that Hilliard should post Father Borowski's. It was Wanda who had let the cat out of the bag. Hilliard was so angry that he couldn't trust himself to speak.

"I didn't do anything wrong, did I? You see, I was pretty sure that Father Borowski's letter didn't contain unused postage stamps like he said it did and that Karminski had only to open it and find a secret message for the fat to be in the fire."

"There's only one thing you forgot and that is that no amount of thought-sending-out or guessing about telephone calls can prevent a political prisoner from being searched." To have told Wanda that he had handed over Father Borowski's letter of his own accord would have meant owning up to his cowardly investigation in DLA PAŃ and that Hilliard wasn't going to do if he could help it. "Fortunately for Father Borowski however the envelope he gave me contained exactly what he said it did: unused Polish postage stamps. Stamps and nothing else. There was no covering letter of any sort."

"That must have been one in the eye for Karminski all right. What did he do? Give the letter back to you again?"

"No; he said that he would have to confiscate the stamps as it was illegal to send them out of Poland, but the offence is so trivial that I expect it'll end there. *De minimis non curat lex*."

"Except in Communist countries. And the Admiral's letter, what did Karminski do with it?"

"He read it of course and then he gave it back to me. There were no unused stamps in the Admiral's letter." Hilliard began to feel happier: at least Wanda's indiscretion had got him out of having to own up to his treachery.

"I don't think that it was because of the unused stamps that Karminski kept Father Borowski's envelope; I think that it was the handwriting he wanted." The snow encrusted windows of a passing tram sent a frail splinter of light quivering across Wanda's glum little face.

"Even if he compared the address with everybody's handwriting in the monastery that still wouldn't tell him who Sardine was; it would only tell him that Father Borowski was the monk who had tried to send unused stamps out of Poland."

"How do you know there wasn't a secret message written in invisible ink under the gum on the flap?"

"There couldn't have been. Before the agent at the other end could read it he would have to wash off the gum and that would mean washing off the invisible ink as well."

"On the envelope itself then—on the inside? Perhaps that's where the secret message was written."

"You and your secret messages! Father Borowski's broken with British Intelligence. If he didn't tell you that he told me. So why on earth should he risk his life sending secret messages? Besides, the letter was addressed to a priest in Scotland—I couldn't help noticing the name when he handed me the envelope."

"There must have been something or we shouldn't both of us be sitting here now. If I'm supposed to be Sardine why didn't Wild Duck even mention the subject? Why didn't he accuse me to my face? The only reason I can think of is that he knew there couldn't be two Sardines as Karminski had told him that it was Father Borowski when he telephoned through to tell him what I'd said about the Admiral's letter. And the reason Karminski knew it was Father Borowski was because of the stamps."

"The stamps couldn't have had anything to do with it— the telephone call had already come through when I was searched."

"And there were no other telephone calls?"

"None incoming. Two outgoing: the first to have plainclothes chaps come in and search me; the second to have that policeman who shoved me into the car beside you come back and fetch me."

"Wild Duck had several incoming ones—I don't know what about because each time all that he kept saying back was *'Tak'*. One of them must have been from one of the plainclothes chaps who searched you."

"What good would that have been when I tell you there was no message in Father Borowski's letter? And what's more the plainclothes chaps weren't in the room when Karminski opened the envelope." But Hilliard was far from feeling as confident as he was trying to sound. There had been that outgoing call about where to look for the Admiral's letter that he couldn't tell Wanda about. How did he know that Karminski hadn't spoken to the policeman about the postage stamps as well? Mightn't there have been a mark on Father Borowski's envelope which Hilliard's untrained eye hadn't noticed? Or mightn't the values of the stamps or the order in which the squares had been arranged have constituted a code? "Perhaps it's just a blanket suspicion they've got against the monastery as a whole," he said as another snowy tram rolled away down the Marszałkowska looking like a lighted shrine. "I can't see how it can possibly be anything precise."

"A blanket suspicion could explain their releasing *me* but not their releasing *you*. What reason did Karminski give for letting *you* go? That he no longer thought that you were Whale?"

"On the contrary he's still so convinced about that, he's expelling me. I'm to leave on the nine-thirty plane tomorrow morning. And to make sure I don't miss it he's coming to the hotel with a car to drive me out to the airport."

"Poor you! But if Karminski still thinks you're Whale then he must still think you know who Sardine is. In that case why hasn't he put you in prison? That's what they generally do with spies they want to find things out from, isn't it?"

"In the best thrillers, yes." The only way to stop Wanda from worrying about Father Borowski was to tell her about his deal with Karminski, and this Hilliard could not bring himself to do: even although his motive had been to save Wanda and the Admiral as well as himself, he knew that Wanda would despise him for having betrayed his country.

"In fact all that either of us can do now is pray."

A rendezvous to say tender goodbys at the seven o'clock Mass in the Kościoł Swiętego Aleksandra struck Hilliard as altogether too blameless an ending to their adventure, and when he had watched the Syrena's tail light diminish into a red tiddlywink at the bottom of the Marszałkowska, he waded hurriedly across the snow to the hotel.

The matchfolder collectors were still making Saturday night whoopee in the restaurant, but Hippolyte found Hilliard a seat in the bar and brought him a bottle of Zubrowka. *"Pamiętasz Capri i nasze spotkanie?"* the cocky little violinist sang. "Do you remember Cap Rye and the lost time we mat?" Halina ballooned past in a yellow dress like a cascade of mayonnaise, staring through Hilliard with smoky pewter eyes. Although he thought this a poor reward for his silence about her part in the currency transaction, Hilliard had too many other cares to bother.

Was even the Dysteleological Surd going to let him get away with treason?

Was Karminski going to keep his word?

Was the Admiral safe?

Was Wanda?

Was Hilliard?

20

As Hilliard's electric razor whirred away like a carpet sweeper in the huge early Sunday morning silence, the sight of his parchmenty face in the mirror made him realize what a fool he had been to imagine that Wanda could ever have fallen in love with him. If he wasn't yet quite Listopad, the month of the falling leaves, he was at least Październik, the month of preparing flax, and much too long in the tooth for Kwiecień, the month of the first blooms. Better Charlotte and her inarticulate bulges, than resemble one of those leathery lechers of sixty riding back from registry offices with mannequins.

There was still no plug on the end of the bath chain so he washed in the basin. Which was perhaps just as well because, what with packing and proving to the floor girl that the zlotys he paid his bill with had not been obtained on the black market, he only just managed to be down in the hall before Wanda arrived to fetch him for Mass. She was wearing the same fantastic rigout as the day before, but it was a cockatoo tuft of red hair and not just a cedilla that was sticking out in front of her jammed on green hat. From her swollen eyelids Hilliard saw that she had been weeping—about Father Borowski, he guessed, not about his own departure.

Outside, it was still dark, but it had stopped snowing, and as they turned into the Hoża bells began to ring out over the pale blue street. The Plac Trzech Krzyży was dappled with worshippers hurrying across the snow and when Wanda and Hilliard entered the church there wasn't a free seat left.

"Don't forget Father Borowski," Wanda said as she knelt on the flagstones between a soldier and an old woman with a

face as lined as the air reconnaissance photograph of a mar-
shaling yard. Hilliard didn't and hoped that for once God
would allow himself to be prodded by a doubting philosopher.

A little later a distant tinkle told Hilliard that Mass had
begun, but all he could see was a flash of green silk now and
then at the altar. Watching the happiness on the faces around
him as they bawled an incomprehensible canticle, Hilliard
wondered if Englishmen could force a Communist Government backed by Soviet tanks to tolerate Protestantism because
of their determination to sing *Abide with Me*.

From the attention with which he was listened to, Hilliard
gathered that the preacher was eloquent. After that there was
more tinkling, the green silk bent and the slim target of the
Host rose for love and betrayal. When they came out on to
the Plac Trzech Krzyży again, the pale blue snow was changing
to heliotrope in the hint of yet another inescapable dawn, and
starlight millions of years old lay dying unconscionably on the
point of Wanda's nose.

"The truce between the Government and the Church is over
apparently, that's what the priest was telling us in his sermon."
An excited black glove flew out like a raven across Hilliard's
face and swooped back to knock the green hat askew and free
another spout of hair. "But he said we mustn't blame the Government too much as it was largely our own fault. He said that
St. Augustine had warned Christians that if they wouldn't go
East to convert the Slavs one day the Slavs would come West
to be converted."

"But the Poles are Slavs too, aren't they?"

"Not the way the Russians are and it's the Russians who are
behind the Government and that's why the priest says it's the
duty of all loyal Poles to stay behind in Poland and convert
the Government and their supporters, if not by word of mouth,
at least by our good example. So perhaps it's just as well I'm
not going to have to be Mrs. Antrobus-Potts."

"I see." But all that Hilliard could see was that Tugboat
Annie had been finally submerged by St. Catherine of Siena.

Truth, he took care not to tell her new missionary face, was elusive, and the enslaved as reluctant as the free to glimpse whatever aspect of it had been glimpsed by the sensitive. In mass conversions the font was inevitably a bandwagon and that was why Christ's coming hadn't made the world a much gentler place than it had been before.

"You still think it's only a blanket suspicion Karminski's got against the monastery?"

"What more can it be?" But Hilliard had now begun to doubt whether he really wanted Karminski's distrust of the monks to be vague: if Karminski didn't know who Sardine was, he might break his word and put Wanda to the question and then it would be only Hilliard's own safety and possibly the Admiral's that his treachery would have purchased.

When they arrived back at the hotel, Hilliard saw that his suitcase was already in the hall. He gave a note to a porter who looked as though he might have brought it down and then went and sat beside Wanda on a small sofa. Two female American matchfolder collectors strode determinedly out to a fresh peal of bells carrying missals with markers as broad as tambourine ribbons.

"We'll keep in touch, won't we?" Hilliard said. "We shan't let the Curtain come between us."

"Unless either of us wants it to it can't."

"And you'll be happy—promise me."

"I promise you that I shall be as happy as I can in a country where most other people are unhappy."

"Your being unhappy too won't make them any happier."

"It will if their unhappiness makes me so unhappy that I do all I can to help them."

Would she still feel the same way at forty, Hilliard wondered. The older one grew the less one dared to see the image. The swing door began to whirl like gin eddying in a cocktail shaker and a few seconds later Karminski was standing in front of them hat in hand.

"I rejoice to see that you have not attempted to do a bunk," he said to Hilliard.

"That would scarcely have been possible. Among thirty million people speaking Polish, a man who doesn't stands out like a sore thumb."

"But perhaps not a man who says that he does not speak Polish and in the vovoidship of Poznań you might have found a green-light floor girl with whom it was money for jam."

Hilliard tried to smile cryptically. He wanted Karminski to think that Wanda and he had been sleeping together. Spies did not slide off islands of fidelity by taking girls to church and the more accessible Karminski thought Wanda, the less likely he would be to imagine she was Sardine.

"Miss Zamoyska can come with us in the car to the airport if she likes. I shall sit in front with the driver so as not to play goosegog."

Hilliard was almost sorry when Wanda accepted: their parting was going to be so painful that he would have preferred to have it over and done with. On her way to the door she tripped over a mat and it was with the comic grin she gave him as she regained her balance that he knew he would always see her until the day he died, with the clock above her green hat at twenty-eight minutes to nine and the lighted tram on the Marszałkowska outside, shining like a Grand Marnier bottle filled with cairngorms.

"Goodby, good come back!" the bootblack who looked like Piłsudski said when Hilliard had given him all his remaining zloty notes barring a few tens he was keeping back for the porter at the airport.

The car was the shape of a catafalque and the driver a policeman with a face as impervious to history as a waterfall or a past participle. Although Karminski sat in front as he had promised, Hilliard was too frightened of a hidden microphone to speak and all he did was to stroke Wanda's fingers through the blunt bag of her fur glove. But when the workers' flats reared up stamped on the scarlet sky as though they were being let down out of heaven, he abandoned caution and said:

"I love you better than anybody I've ever met in my life, I think."

"And however many Dark Nights of the Soul I'm going to have to have to convert the Slavs I'll always love you."

Hilliard saw then how mistaken he had been. Wanda's affection for him was as genuine as her concern for Father Borowski which had only temporarily obscured it. Twenty was the age at which a girl could imagine that love lasted for ever, even love for a man old enough to be her father. At twenty one didn't know that the years eroded the spirit as cruelly as they did the body and that in the long run, the only people who didn't sell the pass were the saints.

"Every night at eight o'clock I'll send you out a thought," Wanda said, "and you'll send me out one. You'll have to remember the difference in time of course. We're an hour ahead of you in winter, I think, but perhaps it'd be safer if you checked."

"I shan't require to: summer or winter I'll be thinking of you all day long."

"And we must both of us be brave when we say goodby at the airport."

But when the time came and Karminski told him that Wanda wouldn't be allowed beyond the barrier, Hilliard's eyes were so misted with tears that he couldn't see her face.

"God bless you, child!" He kissed her on both cheeks and then on the lips. "God bless you and keep you always!"

"God bless you too, *Haroldek*! And now, don't let's either of us look round."

Hilliard did however and the last he saw of her was her green hat bobbing away through the crowd still streaming in through the doorway.

"Every cloud has a silvery lining," Karminski said when they had passed through the customs together and were sitting in the waiting room surrounded by travelers wolfing pastry out of paper bags. "'Age cannot stale her' as your poet says, so for you she will always be an enchanting young dish." He took a manila envelope out of his pocket and handed it to Hilliard. "Here are your dollars and pounds and your friend's list of the Polish months. Count the money if you want to. I am not thin-skinned."

"Thank you, but I don't see any necessity." Hilliard put the envelope away without opening it. If Halina hadn't cheated him, why should Karminski?

"I hope that you will not get in a huff with me if I tell you that I led you up the garden path a little last night. As soon as I was informed that your bath plug had not been replaced I knew that it was that so-called plumber and not Miss Zamoyska who was Sardine. If I had had the sense to have the chain examined a little sooner I might have saved myself much wild goose chasing."

"Wild Duck chasing you mean surely." But Hilliard's mind was only half on his pun. Whom had Karminski sent to examine the chain? Hippolyte of course. Hippolyte was the nigger in the woodpile. Hippolyte, the extra at the British Embassy reception, Hippolyte, the visitor of glorious dead in the Powązki military cemetery, Hippolyte, the swinger of thuribles at Kłock, such apposite ubiquity could only have been planned. Hippolyte had obviously been intruded into the Embassy to spy on the Ambassador as he had been intruded into the monastery to spy on the monks and set to watch Hilliard from the moment of his arrival in Warsaw. Although it could only have been by chance that his first two missions had helped his third, Hippolyte had also been as clever as Hilliard had been stupid.

When the classical bait of a Since October girl hadn't drawn a bite, Hippolyte had used Hilliard's attempt to sell his surplus zlotys instead. The electric light failure at the Manekin had been staged. Halina hadn't been arrested because she had been a decoy. Karminski had only pretended to believe his own upside down version of the exchange deal and propounded the absurd salary charge in the hope of making

Hilliard clear Wanda by denouncing the real Sardine. The Admiral's departure from the reception in the company of the Chinese Ambassador, the letter which Father Borowski had given Hilliard to post in England, in each case the source of Karminski's information must have been Hippolyte. No doubt it was only because he had been held up by the traffic policeman that Hippolyte hadn't arrived in the Powązki military cemetery in time to discover Hilliard in conversation with Sardine, and in the end that hadn't mattered. For if Father Borowski hadn't yet been brought to Warsaw and identified by Karminski as the plug fitting plumber, within the next few hours he would be—Hippolyte couldn't have failed to notice the startled look on Hilliard's face when he had recognized the priest in the sacristy and the agitated shake of the head the priest had given Hilliard. Not only was it all up with Father Borowski, but his plight was largely Hilliard's fault: even if Hilliard had felt that he had to lie to Wanda about the missing bath plug to spare her feelings, with Karminski liable to pop in on him at any moment he ought to have taken the elementary precaution of asking the English speaking concierge to have it replaced.

"Pasażerowie do Moskwy proszeni są do samolotu," a loudspeaker gargled.

"Moscow," Karminski translated as most of the pastry eaters rose and barged towards the gateway. "That was another reason I came along. You are not the sort of person we like to see embarking on the wrong crate."

"Even if I were to, I don't suppose I should get very far as I haven't got a visa."

"You are right. For a clever spy there might be ways and means, but somehow I do not think that you are quite clever enough for that. One last word while there is yet time. Do not lose any beauty sleep about the Admiral. He shall never know that you have shown me his letter."

"So you say. But how do I know that you have not been leading me up the garden path about him like you've been doing about Miss Zamoyska? How do I know that it is not your intention to arrest the Admiral as soon as I have gone?"

"I have kept all the other promises I made you, haven't I? I have given you back your sterling and your dollars and I am allowing you to return to Merrie England even although I know that you are Whale. The only way your superiors can possibly discover our pact will be if *you* fail to keep *your* promise to me and do not post the Admiral's letter. Your Ambassador will not be informed of your expulsion and your publisher will be told that you have had to leave without warning because you received a message from home that your wife had been taken ill."

"You think of everything, don't you?"

"They would chop off my block if I didn't."

Hilliard was too afraid of learning the nature of the secret he had betrayed to risk asking any more questions.

"*Pasażerowie do Londynu i Berlina proszeni są do samolotu.*"

"This time it is for you," Karminski said as he rose. "We shake hands or do we not?"

"Not, I think," Hilliard said and followed the other passengers out across the tarmac.

21

As soon as they had taken off again from East Berlin the air hostess handed out copies of the previous evening's London *Bugle*. What he read there convinced Hilliard that it wasn't only for himself that the days were drawing in, and that it was at Saxons and not at Slavs that Wanda ought to be aiming her Dark Nights of the Soul. He no longer had any qualms of conscience: a country which allowed tycoons and crooners to ride over two generations of its dead soldiers' bones had lost all claim to loyalty. He would carry out his bargain with Karminski and post the Admiral's letter as soon as he arrived in London. If it hadn't been for his loss of Wanda and worry about Father Borowski he might even have contemplated his second act of treason with pleasure.

While he was waiting in the queue at London Airport to have his passport examined, a young man who looked as though he had walked out of an advertisement for Terylene approached Hilliard and asked:

"Professor Hilliard, I presume?"

"Who else?" Was the prophet going to be honored in his own country at last and the Dysteleological Surd reported side by side with film stars' boils?

"Then in that case I'm afraid I must ask you to be kind enough to accompany me."

"Whatever for?" Hilliard could hear the shake in his voice. Karminski must have broken faith with him after all and informed the British Ambassador of his expulsion.

"That, my Master will tell you tomorrow morning. In the meantime however I think I can promise you that we shall make you comfortable. Naturally, I know all this must sound rather cagey but I myself don't carry enough guns to be more explicit."

Guns? Only those who paid others for carrying them talked this way: Royal Army Pay Corps majors and the even smoother operators in Whitehall who controlled them. The alacrity with which the customs officer obeyed the young man's instructions to allow a porter to remove Hilliard's suitcase without examination made it clear to Hilliard that he was up against M.I.5. The shiny black car waiting outside bore the stamp of the Establishment as eloquently as an income tax demand. Only the absence of a policeman with handcuffs enabled him to hope that Karminski hadn't said anything to the Ambassador about the Admiral's letter and that all Hilliard was going to be questioned about was how he had come to be mistaken for Whale.

But as the car glided off as gently as a canoe and the young man sat beside him saying nothing, Hilliard became more and more uneasy. Since the Lonsdale and Blake cases Security had been on its toes. Might not Karminski and Wild Duck have been Polish agents turned British agents and employed to test the loyalty of other British agents in the field? Whale or not Whale, Hilliard was still a British subject and to have shown a British agent's letter to a putative Polish agent was an act of treason at least in intent. Lonsdale had been given twenty-four years, Blake forty-two and their appeals for a reduction of their sentences had been rejected. How long would they give a Professor of Logic and Metaphysics cowardly enough not to have behaved like the British agent he had been mistaken for? Five years? Five months would be more than enough if all that the Sunday newspapers said about beatings up were true.

One thing at least was certain: whatever the charge brought against him, to be found with the Admiral's letter in his possession would be fatal. This, to prevent pulling it out by mistake with his passport, he was carrying in the right hand side pocket of his jacket. The Terylene young man was sitting on his left. Provided Hilliard's movements were unobtrusive enough he might be able to slide the letter down the window well as he had in the Syrena when Wanda and he had been arrested outside Toruń. If he brought it off, the odds were that the letter would never be found, not even when the car was sent to the junk yard to be broken up, and by then the sleuths would probably have forgotten that they had ever carried Hilliard as a passenger.

"I find those ghastly little primrose and pale blue doors rather unnerving, don't you?" The young man pointed out at the ugly villas sliding past like a string of dinosaur's droppings. "A copy of *Decline and Fall* on the top of the telephone directory would be a more convincing status symbol, don't you think?"

"The only originality that's tolerated these days is its reflection." Two moves would do it: first the letter from his pocket, then the letter to the well.

"I couldn't disagree with you less. If the Dean were to lead Maggie up St. Paul's with a chamberpot on her tresses all the gals would roll up for Ascot under jerries. Look, Professor Hilliard, I hate to nip initiative in the bud, but *my* right hand is in *my* right side pocket and if you go on trying to insert *your* right hand into your *right* side pocket I shall be forced to commit what we call an Unavowable Activity. When I said I didn't carry enough guns I was speaking metaphorically."

After so menacing a statement Hilliard expected to be blindfolded as soon as they reached the outskirts of London, but apparently M.I.5 disdained the secretive methods employed by its opposite number in Warsaw. The car was driven straight to a block of flats near Manchester Square where Hilliard was taken up to a suite on the third floor as devoid of personality as a dish of Brussels sprouts.

"The question is: do I search or do you forthcome?" the

138

young man asked when the chauffeur had dumped Hilliard's suitcase in the entrance hall and departed.

"I forthcome of course." For the first time in his life Hilliard felt grateful to Charlotte for having nagged him into carrying nothing in his side pockets which could make them bulge. His passport, air ticket folder, wallet and Karminski's envelope were all in his inside breast pocket, and these he handed to the young man, adding his handkerchief when he remembered it.

"Of course foreign currency is really the Treasury's pigeon, but I presume it was your intention to exchange all these jolly little dollars for sterling at some authorized bank."

"Was and is."

"Anything else for me to look shameful about for prying into?"

"Nothing."

"Are you sure? What about that revolver you were going to shoot your way to freedom to read *The News of the World* in bed on Sunday morning with?"

"I have no revolver."

"No revolver? Then in that case you must have a pipe. Even in the anti-novel the anti-hero can't get away with threatening the anti-policeman unless he's got a revolver or a pipe." The young man's hands were into Hilliard's side pockets and out again before he had finished speaking and in one of them was the Admiral's letter. "'Director of Naval Intelligence'—that's reassuring: I didn't know the fellow could read."

"Of course now you're going to believe the worst of me and I can't altogether blame you."

"The believing or disbelieving is up to my Master. Normally he would have seen you right away, but as today's Sunday and he's worshipping God in one of those green cathedrals with eighteen holes in it I'm afraid you'll have to put up with my company till tomorrow morning. Fortunately there's plenty of reading matter: *Religio Medici, The Anatomy of Melancholy,*

A la Recherche du Temps Perdu on the shelves and *The Ladies' Directory* in the fridge—*video meliora, proboque; deteriora sequor*. And when I've committed the impropriety of routing through your suitcase I'll see if I can rustle up some fish and chips."

Next morning after a sleepless night in the same bedroom as the young man and a breakfast he scarcely touched, Hilliard was shown into an office in which a middle-aged man with an esplanade of bald head and eyes that bulged like poached eggs was sitting alone at a desk. Strewn across the blotting pad, like washing waiting to be ironed, were Hilliard's passport, air ticket folder, wallet, sterling and dollar notes, Wanda's list of the Polish months, two newspapers and the Admiral's letter, slit open.

"I apologize for any inconvenience which we may have caused you, Professor Hilliard, but in these days of apostasy in high places we make a point of interrogating all persons of prominence who have decried our Western Way of Life while they were abroad as soon as they return to England." Bald Pate stood one of the newspapers on end so that Hilliard could see the title *Polska Prawda*. "While we do not wish to interfere with the right of our intellectuals to express their political opinions, we nevertheless feel it our duty to point out to them that by doing so in potentially hostile countries, they are taking the shortest cut possible to not being able to express them anywhere."

"You've got me all wrong, sir," Hilliard said, wondering how he was going to wriggle out of it when Bald Pate got round to the Admiral's letter. "I am not a Communist and I haven't the slightest intention of ever becoming one. The reason I flew off the handle the way I did was because both the British Ambassador and the British Council thought up phoney excuses so as to be able to get out of attending a lecture I had been invited to give in Warsaw."

"Whatever official discourtesy you were subjected to scarcely warranted a public commendation of the defection of Burgess and Maclean. You see, Professor Hilliard, after all these recent rumblings it's *secret* conversions that we have to be most on our guard against and that is why Mr. Worthington-Truscott met you at the airport and brought you straight to this flat. If nothing compromising had been found on your person I should merely have admonished you and that would have been the end of the matter. Unfortunately however. . . ." The poached eyes swiveled round towards the pile of banknotes with such a jerk that it looked as though they were about to drop out of their sockets and go rolling across the table like billiard balls. "Those dollars and those pounds, Professor Hilliard—just how do you come to be in the possession of so much money?"

"I did an illegal swop of the zloty royalties my Polish publisher paid me in Warsaw—illegal in Poland, that is." That furrowed waistcoat, that rainstained Homburg perched like a brooding hen on the hatstand, were these the vestments of pontifical skulduggery?

"And with whom did you do this illegal swop?"

"With a girl in a bar. You'll find the calculations on the back of that list of the months in Polish you've got lying there."

"Thank you. I had already seen them." The billiard balls swerved towards the Admiral's letter so sharply that Hilliard felt he ought to have heard a click. "And this letter addressed to the Director of Naval Intelligence—just how did you come by *it*?"

"Admiral Sir David Doddick was staying in the same hotel as I was in Warsaw and he asked me to post the letter for him when I got back to England as he said he had still to go on to Kraków and Częstochowa and didn't like the idea of posting it in Poland in case it might be opened by the censorship. He was over there for an International Matchfolder Collectors' Convention and I used to run into him in the restaurant and bars."

"And in which did the Admiral give you the letter to post—in a restaurant or in a bar?"

"In neither. In the sacristy of a monastery at a place called Kłock."

"Then it wasn't only in restaurants and bars that you ran into the Admiral; it was in restaurants and bars and sacristies."

"And also in a cemetery."

"Let's get your evidence correct then, shall we? While you were in Poland you met Admiral Sir David Doddick in restaurants and bars and sacristies and cemeteries and in one of the sacristies he gave you a letter addressed to the Director of Naval Intelligence which he asked you to post for him as soon as you returned here to England."

"I only met the Admiral in one restaurant and in one bar and in one sacristy and in one cemetery."

"Bars *au pluriel*, you said if I remember rightly."

"I was talking generically."

"In that case why were you not also talking generically about the restaurant and the sacristy and the cemetery?"

"Because there was a bar so near the hotel restaurant that you could almost say it formed part of it and because I also ran into the Admiral in another bar outside."

"I understand. After all there could scarcely have been a sacristy and a cemetery as well as a bar attached to the hotel restaurant, could there?" If Bald Pate were joking there was no sign of it in his expression, and Hilliard realized that the only way he could hope to avoid prison was to tell Bald Pate as much of the truth as was possible.

As briefly as he could therefore, Hilliard summarized his misadventures: the blunders about the suitcase and the overcoat which had led Karminski and his friend Wild Duck to imagine that he was a British agent called Whale; the searching of his luggage as soon as he had arrived in Warsaw; Wanda's unsuccessful attempt to have his missing bath plug replaced by telepathy; Halina's offer to give him dollars and pounds in exchange for his surplus zloty royalties; MacOgg and his shirts; Sardine's visit and his plumber act with Karminski; his second meeting with Sardine in the cemetery; his conversation with the British Ambassador and the interpretation Karminski had put upon the Admiral's departure from the reception in the company of the Chinese Ambassador; the seizure of Halina's dollars and pounds at the Manekin and Karminski's pretending that it was them Hilliard had been trying to exchange in order to be able to pay Wanda her spy's salary in zlotys; his visit to the monastery with Wanda and his astonishment at discovering that Sardine was Father Borowski; the letter which Father Borowski as well as the Admiral had given him to post in England; Wild Duck's appearances at Drujsk and Kłock; Father Borowski's plan to have Anchovy extrude Wanda and Hilliard to England as Mr. and Mrs. Antrobus-Potts; his failure to tumble to the significance of Hippolyte's ubiquity; the arrest outside Toruń and the drive back to Warsaw. Bald Pate listened to the whole story in silence until Hilliard came to his final interrogation by Karminski.

"And of course you couldn't stop his finding both letters on you when he had you searched?"

"I didn't even try to stop him finding Father Borowski's. In fact I handed it over of my own accord. Father Borowski had told me there were only unused Polish stamps in it and I wanted to pull the wool over Karminski's eyes if I could."

"How could you be sure that Father Borowski was telling you the truth? How did you know there wasn't a top secret message inside?"

"For the simple reason that I had taken the trouble to check. A suspect like myself couldn't afford to be caught carrying anything incriminating, so before we left Toruń I went into the lavatory and opened the envelope with the point of my Biro. When I saw that there were only stamps inside I sealed it down again."

"And the Admiral's letter? Did you open that too? Or didn't you think the address incriminating enough?"

"Of course I did. And I was going to open the letter to make sure. But just as I was about to do so somebody began to bang on the lavatory door so I threw it into the w.c. and pulled the plug but unfortunately it didn't work properly and I had to fish the letter out again and put it back in my pocket."

"These continental privies do tend to become somewhat inarticulate at times, don't they?"

"However, it wasn't Wild Duck as naturally I'd feared but only the waiter who wanted to tell me that I'd gone into the *Damski* in mistake for the *Męski* because the *Damski* and the *Męski* hadn't been called the *Damski* and the *Męski* but *Dla* something or other each instead."

"We once lost an agent in Budapest that way: in Hungarian the only difference is a diaeresis."

"So when we were arrested suddenly like that, the only thing I could think of was to shove the letter down the window well before the policeman hauled us out of the car and pushed us into the back seat."

"That was resourceful of you. But in that case how does the letter still come to be in your possession?"

Hilliard then told Bald Pate about Wanda's attempt to make Wild Duck believe that it was only the Admiral who had given Hilliard a letter to post in England; about Wild Duck's telephoning this information through to Karminski; about the second failure of Wanda's telepathy and his own insistence that it was only the priest who had given him a letter to post in England; about the brutality with which he had been searched and Karminski's threatening him with torture if he didn't reveal where he had hidden the Admiral's letter.

"And so naturally you sold the pass?"

The moment of untruth was upon Hilliard at last. However much those searchlight eyes might make him feel he was made of glass and that Bald Pate was reading down into the sour lies curdling in his belly, he must not let himself be beguiled into admitting that he had committed treason.

"No, sir, I didn't. Whether I should have sold it in the end I can't honestly say because luckily for me I was never put to the test. Just as Karminski was saying that he would give me five minutes to think things over a policeman who must have been searching the Syrena came in with the letter and handed it to Karminski."

"A *deus ex machina* indeed! Even so how does it happen that you are now back in England with all this loot?" The bulging eyes were held over the dollar and pound notes like magnifying glasses. "Karminski was still convinced you were Whale, wasn't he?"

"But a brave Whale, sir—at least that's how Karminski put it. He said that as a spy himself he knew how to appreciate courage in another spy when he saw it. An exaggeration perhaps, because as I've already said I'm not at all sure I'd have been able to stick to my guns if I'd been given what I understand you call the treatment. Anyway not only did he say that he would let me go and give me my money back but he also promised to take no steps against either Miss Zamoyska or the Admiral. Of course letting me go was really expelling me as my visa wasn't up for another five days and what's more he came to the airport himself to make sure that I didn't try to dodge the plane." Hilliard tried to believe that this distortion didn't sound so very much more implausible than the truth.

"Expelling you was a kindness as far as Worthington-Truscott was concerned: you've no idea how tired the poor chap got meeting all those Lot planes. You see, we knew you weren't traveling BEA and it was against the drill for us to ask Polskie Linie Lotnicze when you had booked your return passage. However don't let's get entangled." The magnifying glasses had become the popping lenses of telescopes adjusted to scan prevarications tearing Hilliard's mouth like bricks. "Weren't you at all worried about leaving Miss Zamoyska behind? How could you be sure that Karminski wouldn't go back on his word and arrest her as soon as you had left?"

"I couldn't, sir—not until Karminski told me at the airport that he had found out that my bath plug hadn't been replaced and then it was no longer Miss Zamoyska but Father Borowski that I was worried about."

"And the Admiral? Had you no qualms about him?"

"Plenty, sir, but there was absolutely nothing I could do about them. The Admiral didn't say *when* he was leaving for Kraków or Częstochowa or which he was going to visit first, but even if I had known for certain that he was still in Kłock I couldn't have risked telephoning him in case the line were tapped, and writing would have been even more dangerous. Going to prison myself wouldn't have helped him either because if Karminski really intended to arrest him he would have done so whether I was locked up or not."

"And this letter of his? What were you supposed to do with it? Post it here as though nothing had happened?"

"That was Karminski's idea certainly, but I can assure you that it wasn't mine. If circumstances hadn't prevented me I was going to have taken it round to the Admiralty first thing in the morning and asked to see the Director of Naval Intelligence and told him the whole story."

"In that case why did you attempt to get rid of the letter on your way here from the airport? I presume you were trying to do the same thing as you say that you did in the Syrena when you were arrested—push it down the window well? If you can tell me the truth why couldn't you tell it to Worthington-Truscott?"

"Because I lost my head, that's all. As I've already told Mr. Worthington-Truscott I thought that M.I.5 had got to hear of my being mistaken for Whale and I didn't want there to be any risk of their thinking that I'd been up to mischief. Put yourself in my position, sir, and I think you'll understand."

"I do indeed. With both the Admiral's letter and all that money in your possession people might get all sorts of funny ideas into their heads."

That he had been paid by Karminski for having shown him the Admiral's letter, was that what Bald Pate was insinuating? Already Hilliard could see the headlines:

PROFESSOR SELLS BRITAIN'S DEFENCE SECRETS
EX-ROYAL ARMY PAY CORPS PRIVATE IN TOWER

"But those calculations, sir—you told me you'd seen them. The first represents my agents' commission at the official rate of sixty-seven zlotys worked out at the black market rate of two hundred zlotys to the pound which was what the girl said she was going to give me for my zlotys. And the ninety-five thousand zlotys from which the product is subtracted are my zloty royalties less ten thousand for my expenses in Warsaw. The dollars and pounds you have there are what the girl gave me for them at seventy to the dollar and two hundred to the pound. If you don't believe me ring up my agents. Catacomb and Priddle's the name—you'll find them in the book."

"I have no need to ring up anybody, Professor Hilliard. Funnily enough the money's one of the two things which convinces me that your rocambolesque tale is true." The severity on Bald Pate's knobbly face was breaking up like lumps of thawing snow about to slide off a roof. "And what you have just told me confirms it. You say that you were exchanging ninety-five thousand zlotys into pounds and dollars at two hundred zlotys to the pound and seventy to the dollar. You have here one thousand dollars which at seventy makes seventy thousand zlotys. Which means that in order to make up the remaining twenty-five thousand zlotys this Halina would have required to give you £125. Instead of which you have here only £120 : 5 : 0 as no doubt you have already remarked."

"As a matter of fact, sir, I hadn't. From what Karminski said I gathered that there might be a slight shortage, but I didn't like to check at the airport for fear of hurting his feelings and on the plane I had other things on my mind."

"Then you will be interested to learn that the difference of

£4 : 15 : 0 is accounted for by this check for five shillings which your lady friend's ignorance of the English language must have deluded her into accepting as five pounds." The check which Bald Pate handed Hilliard was drawn on the Bank of St. Monans and Pittenweem. It was made out to bearer and signed Hector MacOgg.

"Of all the dirty tricks!" Hilliard said when his amusement had subsided.

"Quite apart from the fact that foreign agents never pay traitors by check and if they did, would be careful not to cheat them, the fraud is of a piece with that you have already told me about Mr. MacOgg and his shirts. It also substantiates your statement that he remained behind in the Café Manekin with this otherwise apparently highly successful hetaera when you and the Admiral went on to the reception at the British Embassy. But a still better reason for believing you is provided by the Admiral's letter itself."

The letter which Bald Pate took out of the slit envelope and handed to Hilliard read:

"My dear Chips,

From what 'a Chinese Spokesman' here in Warsaw tells me Polaris comes too late in the day to make Mao or Chou think they would gain anything by swopping horses in midstream. So if I were in your oilskins I'd order a mass sit-down of the ratings at Aldermaston because turning the other cheek in time seems the only way out of this mess for the West. Meanwhile I'm off to Częstochowa to find out how the Pauline monks there repelled a Swedish invasion of Poland in 1665 by prayer so that we can at least set about preparing to win the next war but one.

In haste,

Your ole Sparring Partner,
Tomato"

"We haven't yet sunk to employing Sinbads insecure enough to mention the function of their Masters on envelopes enclosing reports from the field," Bald Pate went on when Hilliard had given him back the letter. "Not only is the Admiral not an

148

agent, but he doesn't even know that such a person as Sardine exists. His visit to Kłock therefore can only have been what he told you it was: a private visit to an old school chum of his son's. Not in Karminski's eyes though: to Karminski his turning up in the sacristy with Sardine and yourself must have been the last nail in poor old Tomato's coffin. And if anything besides the address were required to convince him that this typical piece of retired naval hysteria was an authentic report from an agent in the field it must have been your disposal of the letter when you were arrested and denial that you had ever received it. Unfortunately however as on your own admission you were never actually *subjected* to torture we can't very well put you up for a George Cross or Medal. And a knighthood 'for distinguished services to philosophy' is out because when all is said and done you did make those rather snide remarks on the other side of the Curtain, didn't you?"

"Yes, sir, I'm afraid I did." Instead of the Tower it was the New Year's Honors List that he seemed to have escaped. Baffled, Hilliard waited for Bald Pate to continue.

"That Sardine has come to share your views doesn't surprise me as it's more than six months since we last had a cheep out of him. Silence in our line of business is not always golden so we decided to send Whale out to investigate. Our Whale was a literary gent too and we warned Sardine to be prepared for his visit. That's why Sardine made the same mistake as Karminski who must have been tipped off by some bleak Blake still blushing unseen in the corridors and council chambers of M.I.5. Up to now our cover story has always been the export drive, but as we thought that was getting slightly shopsoiled we decided to stick to the truth for a change."

"So that's why the Ambassador thought I was Whale too?"

"Precisely. All we told Nodder this time was that an agent called Whale was in the pipeline—he says the less he knows about the details the easier it is for him to pretend he doesn't know anything at all. The taking off dates too were almost the same—the real Whale left yesterday morning. However he ought to be able to get back all right now that Karminski thinks he's expelled him—unless of course he doesn't realize that Sardine's blown and does something silly like going and ringing the bell at Kłock. That missing bath plug of yours did the trick all right as you'll realize from this paragraph here."

The blue penciled lines in *The Daily Telegraph* read:

POLISH PRIEST GAOLED FOR CURRENCY OFFENCE.

Warsaw, Sunday.

Father Jan Borowski, a monk at Kłock, was arrested today on the charge of having conspired with an agent of a foreign Power to speculate against the zloty.

"Unused stamps!" Hilliard was so shocked that he almost failed to notice that the winter sunlight was slowly transforming Bald Pate's head into a melon. "And it was I who handed them over!"

"Even if you hadn't they'd still have found them when they searched you. And in any case the stamps were only a pretext. It was the bath plug that gave the show away and that wasn't your fault either."

But Hilliard was far from being sure that it wasn't and he could feel his face turning as grey as his hair with shame.

"And at least, Professor Hilliard, you have the satisfaction of knowing that you have been instrumental in throwing a great deal of dust in the eyes of our potential enemies. For we *are* trying to split the Communist Church. The only mistake Karminski made was to imagine that we should be stupid enough to choose Warsaw as the setting for our conversation piece and a garrulous wencher like Doddick as our plenipotentiary. The reason I'm telling you this is to ease your conscience and you are under the same obligation as Worthington-Truscott and myself to repeat it to nobody."

"I understand, sir."

"Another thing. However much you may feel tempted to tell your wife or your friends about your adventures I must ask you to keep them to yourself—for the sake of the Western

Slide to Death." Bald Pate showed a necklace of pale green teeth in what looked almost like a smile.

"You may count on me, sir. You're Caviare, sir, aren't you."

"*Toujours* under the Official Secrets Act, you may think of me as Bloater."

On the whole it was perhaps just as well that he was not going to be allowed to talk, Hilliard reflected as he watched Worthington-Truscott slide his suitcase into the taxi: Charlotte would never have forgiven him for the missed knighthood.

"Whatever that eminent poltroon up there may have told you," Worthington-Truscott said through the window, "Tomato's right: we've had it. If I may be allowed to make an Unavowable *Statement,* Franco's the boy for *my* money. O all ye works of the Blimps, bless ye the Blimps: praise them, and magnify them for ever!"

22

"£298 : 9 : 0 I thought we'd agreed upon," Catacomb said.

"*You* thought we'd agreed upon," Hilliard corrected. "Two hundred to the pound was the most I could get for my zlotys on the black market in Warsaw and two hundred to the pound is all you're going to get for your commission. 19,996 zlotys at two hundred to the pound works out at £99 : 19 : 7½d, but for good measure I've given you one hundred pounds so I don't see you've got anything to grumble about." A man who had been through what Hilliard had been through was no longer going to let himself be bilked by a Catacomb. A man who had just seen a knighthood slip under his nose deserved £370 : 5 : 0 not to tell the Inland Revenue about instead of only £176 : 11 : 0.

"Of course I see your point of view," Catacomb said meekly.

"You've not only got to see it; you've got to accept it. And in case you haven't noticed there's a check there." Hilliard smiled as he pictured MacOgg's consternation when he saw the five shillings he thought he'd buried for ever on the Rynek Starego Miasta rising from the dead in his St. Monans and Pittenweem passbook. "If you think it'll bounce get rid of it on Gumshott."

"Gumshott's over in Warsaw too now as a matter of fact. Pulled out yesterday morning. Apparently he's found a character there who says he can bring pressure to bear on publishers to remit in sterling instead of pretending that the National Bank of Poland won't play. Chap by the name of Borowski. You didn't happen to run into him by any chance? Borowski, I mean, not Gumshott."

Who'd have believed it? The tears of things, the tears of things! If Gumshott didn't get back safely the only thing for Hilliard to do was to hope that the sub-agent was as loathsome as Catacomb.

"Anyway don't forget what I told you. *Forever Mellors, No Bonds for James Amber*, sex or violence, that's the royal road to a villa in the south of France. Sorry to chase you, Harold, but I've got another of our authors pawing the ground outside. I quite understand about the commission so don't lose any sleep about it."

"Don't worry—I shan't." Hilliard was still grinning with triumph when he arrived at St. Pancras. Charlotte was right: the only way to get on in this world was to throw your weight about.

Charlotte herself however looked as though she were going to be a much tougher nut to crack than Catacomb.

"Just what I was afraid of: you've gone and got fat again. I'll have to put you on another diet. Starting from tomorrow though: the Scroggies are coming round for dinner. And I see you've got a sock on inside out for a change."

But after she had finished unpacking for him and blown him up for not having used the return luggage label she had written out for him, Hilliard had a few minutes by himself in the bedroom in which to try to re-think the shape of his dull world.

Two nights ago he had been dining with Wanda in Toruń, that was how he was going to have to count time from now on, six nights ago, eighteen months ago, five years ago. Over the humps of platitudinous roofs the town clock began to strike seven. It was the hour for Sending Out Thoughts. Was Wanda trying to tell him as he was trying to tell Wanda about the Dark Nights of the Soul they were both of them going to have for ever about Father Borowski?

He took out her list of the Polish months, kissed it and put it back in his wallet. Then he went down to greet the Professor of Accounting and his wife.

 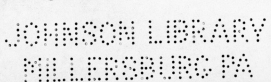